# SWEETWATER

# ALSO BY LAURENCE YEP

## GOLDEN MOUNTAIN CHRONICLES

The extraordinary intergenerational story of the Young family from Three Willows Village, Kwangtung province, China, and their lives in the Land of the Golden Mountain — America.

The Serpent's Children (1849)

Mountain Light (1855)

Dragon's Gate (1867)
*A Newbery Honor Book*

The Traitor (1885)

Dragonwings (1903)
*A Newbery Honor Book*

The Red Warrior (1939)
*Coming soon*

Child of the Owl (1965)

Sea Glass (1970)

Thief of Hearts (1995)

## DRAGON OF THE LOST SEA FANTASIES

Dragon of the Lost Sea

Dragon Steel

Dragon Cauldron

Dragon War

## THE TIGER'S APPRENTICE TRILOGY

The Tiger's Apprentice

Tiger's Blood
*Coming soon*

Tiger Magic
*Coming soon*

When the Circus Came to Town

The Dragon Prince

Dream Soul

The Imp That Ate My Homework

The Magic Paintbrush

The Rainbow People

The Star Fisher

## CHINATOWN MYSTERIES

The Case of the Goblin Pearls

The Case of the Lion Dance

The Case of the Firecrackers

## EDITED BY LAURENCE YEP

American Dragons: *Twenty-Five Asian American Voices*

# LAURENCE YEP

# SWEETWATER

HARPERCOLLINS*PUBLISHERS*

www.harperchildrens.com

Library of Congress Cataloging-in-Publication Data

Yep, Laurence.

Sweetwater / by Laurence Yep ; map by Julia Noonan.

p.   cm.

Originally published: New York : Harper & Row, 1973.

Summary: A boy and his people, colonists on the planet Harmony, try to save their way of life.

ISBN 0-06-056028-2 — ISBN 0-06-056029-0 (pbk.)

[1. Science fiction.]  I. Noonan, Julia, ill.  II. Title.

PZ7.Y44Sw 2004

[Fic]—dc21

2003047873

Typography by Karin Paprocki

1  2  3  4  5  6  7  8  9  10

❖

*To*
FRANCINE ANN,
LISA MARIE,
MICHAEL THOMAS,
AND KATHY SUE
FOR THEIR PATIENCE.

# CONTENTS

| | INTRODUCTION | ix |
|---|---|---|
| 1 | THE GREAT SILKIE | 1 |
| 2 | THE PRICE OF A SONG | 25 |
| 3 | THE SONS OF LIGHT | 45 |
| 4 | THE GARDEN | 65 |
| 5 | THE NIGHT VIGIL | 79 |
| 6 | THE TOUCHSTONE | 91 |
| 7 | SATIN'S TEMPTATION | 103 |
| 8 | THE RUNAWAY | 117 |
| 9 | STREET OF GOLD | 133 |
| 10 | SION'S WALLS | 147 |
| 11 | "SIMPLE GIFTS" | 159 |
| 12 | THE SEADRAGON | 173 |
| | EPILOGUE: SOME LOOSE THREADS | 187 |

# INTRODUCTION

I BEGAN MY professional writing career not as a writer of Chinese American stories but of science fiction. As a young reader, there were only a few Chinese American writers in print and none of their books were for children.

Instead, what I read—devoured might be more accurate—were science fiction and fantasy. I had grown up in an Afro-American neighborhood of San Francisco and went to a Catholic school in Chinatown. Because all I knew was life in two different ghettos, the so-called realistic books about life in the suburbs seemed like fantasies to me.

I identified with fantasy and science fiction because, in fantasy and science fiction, you have children taken from our everyday world to a different place where they have to learn new customs and a new language. Science fiction talked about adapting, and that's something I did every time I got on and off the bus.

In those days, the librarians in San Francisco would fix a little blue rocket to the spine of such books, and I would walk down the stacks, picking out anything with that precious symbol. I still remember my delight when I would discover a new Andre Norton novel, for it meant I could explore yet another universe she had created. As grim as they could be, I was drawn to her worlds in crisis, in which old ways were coming crashing down to be replaced by new—and not necessarily better—ones.

The other science-fiction writer for whom I always hunted was Robert Heinlein, for it meant I could meet another one of his humorous, often self-deprecating narrators. I especially loved how, in the space of a few paragraphs of a first-person narrative, the character came to life and was so engaging that I wanted to accompany him or her across a galaxy.

Yet as much as science fiction and fantasy formed the literary backbone of my childhood, I never expected to write any. Then, in my senior year in high school, I had an English teacher, Reverend John Becker, S.J., who delighted in challenging his students. He took some of us aside and said if we wanted to get an A in his course, we had to get something accepted by a national magazine. He later retracted his threat; as long as we could show him our rejection letters, he graded us the way he did the rest of the class.

However, I realized that though a rejection letter could depress me, it did not destroy me, and so I kept sending out stories. It wasn't until I went to school at Marquette University in Milwaukee that I first tried my hand at science fiction, at the age of eighteen. Feeling terribly homesick, I was able to return home in mind if not in body. I wrote a science-fiction story in which San Francisco had sunk underneath the ocean after an earthquake. To my amazement, I sold that story, "The Selchey Kids," to a pulp magazine, *The Worlds of If*. (It was later anthologized in *World's Best Science Fiction of 1969*.)

I subsequently wrote more science fiction; but when I was

in graduate school in Buffalo, a friend, Joanne Ryder (whom I later married), had become an editor in children's books at Harper & Row, and she asked me to write some science fiction for children.

I was feeling homesick once more, and so writing was again a vehicle to take me home. As happens with so many of my books, it began by describing an image that, though it was imaginary, seemed so real that I felt as if I were simply describing a picture that was projected on an inner screen. Within my mind, I saw a boy lying on the floor of his living room gazing up as the sunlight, bouncing off the water in the street outside, sent reflections rippling across the ceiling.

It was the last calm moment he was to have for, as in one of Andre Norton's novels, his own world was about to reach a crisis that would change it forever. It also seemed natural to write as if he were speaking directly to the reader as Heinlein's narrators did.

And since simultaneous with writing *Sweetwater* I was also studying Mark Twain and other period writers in graduate school, I wound up giving a pioneering nostalgia to the novel that, I hope, tints the atmosphere like the sepia hue of an old photograph.

That same impulse led me to give Biblical names to most of the human characters since that was a common practice in early America. One of the exceptions was Tyree, whose name either came from a *Star Trek* episode or a John Wayne movie— which probably reflects my twin interests.

It was only several years later, after I had begun writing the Golden Mountain Chronicles, that I looked back at *Sweetwater* and my other science fiction and realized that even then I had been writing about myself as a Chinese American. In my adult science fiction, I had either written about alienated heroes or even the first-person narratives of aliens themselves. Through fiction, I had been exploring my own feelings of being an outsider.

*Sweetwater* was the next step in comprehending my Chinese American identity. At the time I wrote the novel, it seemed perfectly logical to me that Argans should be uncles and nephews and cousins, though I could not have explained why; and yet when I thought about it afterward I realized the society of the Argans reflected the society of Chinatown at the turn of the century, which because of harsh immigration laws was populated mostly by males who would be uncles, nephews, and cousins to one another. Those Chinese Americans had made their own contributions to their world just as Amadeus shares music with Tyree.

I also began to realize that the crisis that hits Tyree's world— and in general my own fascination with Andre Norton—was a reflection of boyhood. When I was young, both Chinatown and my own neighborhood were in transition physically, socially, and culturally, and beyond that the conflict between old and new ways mirrored what I experienced every day as a child of two cultures.

I think that also explains why *Sweetwater*, like most of my adult science fiction, was set where the land meets the sea. Tyree, like my other early heroes, was comfortable not only on the land but on or in the sea as well. Their amphibiousness was a physical symbol of what it was like to move back and forth between two different cultures; and so, in giving dual natures to my heroes, I was attempting to understand what I felt being the product of both Chinese and American cultures.

In a box in my study is a half-finished sequel to *Sweetwater* in which Tyree and his family journey southward to an undersea archaeological dig, but I have never been able to finish it. In part, I am no longer the person who, more than thirty years ago, wrote *Sweetwater*. Perhaps it's also because I began exploring my Chinese American roots directly in *Dragonwings*, *Dragon's Gate*, and the other Golden Mountain Chronicles, and so I no longer feel an inner compulsion to do it indirectly in science fiction. Yet, without *Sweetwater*, I'm not sure I would have had the courage to have begun that journey into Chinese America in the first place.

*Laurence Yep*

The Spaceport

Sheol

Silkies Take
Refuge here
from Seadragon

Priests'
Private
Fish Run

To New Sion

Coastline
in dry
years

Satin's Ship hovers here

Priests'
Garden

Avicenna    Avenue

Arimeth    Street

Tarsus    Street

Terran Way

The Commune

Main
Fish Run

N
W    E
S

"Map of Old Sion"

# 1

## THE GREAT SILKIE

THE GALAXY IS an awfully big place so I don't expect you to know about my home world, Harmony; but my ancestors came from Earth. If you go out some cold winter night and look for your constellation Virgo, you might be able to see the tiny pinprick of light on her left side where her heart ought to be. That's my star, but even if you strained your eyes, you wouldn't be able to see the fifth planet around that star, which is my world.

It's a hard life on a star colony and most humans are too busy trying to survive even to learn where Earth is in the night sky, but that was one of the first things Pa taught me. Pa said that at least his son would remember Earth. He said that in each generation one of us must be able to tell the others about the old Earth ways, and I guess he was right.

But I think it's just as important that we don't forget our city, Old Sion, now that we're about to leave it, and I think it's even more important that we remember how we lost it. Pa says that no one person's responsible, but I figure Pa's just being nice. If I hadn't wanted to play the flute or go mixing with aliens, we wouldn't have had so much trouble. Anyway,

I'm going to try to write about what happened during the last few years. And maybe, just maybe, I can save something of what we're losing—for the generations to come on Harmony and for you people back on Earth who don't know what it's like to live on a star colony.

The first thing you ought to know is that our colony here was split into two groups, the ones we call the Mainlanders and my own group, the Silkies. You see, the original colony built a city on what they thought was the coast; but Harmony has a fifty-year cycle of tides and they built Old Sion during the lowest time of the tides. When the sea rose, half submerging the city, a lot of the colonists gave up and moved to the mountain ranges twenty miles to the east where they *knew* it would be dry and built a new city, called New Sion.

But my ancestors stayed on in the city, learning to adjust to the new kind of life, traveling about in the flooded streets in boats. They took so well to the half-flooded city that the other colonists began to call my ancestors Silkies. The Mainlanders meant it as an insult because the mythical Silkies were so ugly on the land, but my ancestors adopted the name with pride because the Silkies were beautiful in their own mysterious sea.

From the very day the colony was founded, my ancestors had never gotten along with the other colonists. My ancestors had been the crews of the starships that had brought the colonists here, and they had never intended to stay; but when their starships broke down, they were stranded. Because of their different background and because of pride, they stayed apart from the other colonists.

And these lonely men fell in love with a city no one else wanted. Each family of Silkies took a house, salvaging more

than enough to make their homes comfortable. A lot of the
former residents just left things—like chairs and tables—
intending to come back for them later and then forgetting

n Pa found them in a
ed basement.
escent mosses, and they
ned the flooded alleys
rubble and then stock-
eaweed. (Of course, the
exactly like the kinds
ames to their counter-
v fat in the slack water
eeping them inside the
useholds used the food
eir diet; but their main

from the sea up a river
ainland. That was real-
turned to gold. It was
ill the hard months by
But don't let me give
nt a lot of hard work,
ted.
he whole Commune
ind sing and dance—
everyone, that is, except my father. Ever since my father was
elected Captain, he hated to be seen wasting time. Though my
parents liked music, Pa didn't think they ought to show it in
public. Ma's got a beautiful voice but Pa and my little sister
Caley and I were about the only ones who got to hear her.

During the winter fête, Pa always made us sit on the side, backs straight against the wall, smiling solemnly while the other folks had fun. It was like Pa didn't want the other Silkies to think he was frivolous. I asked him one time about Great-Great-Grandpa Lamech, who was not only the first Captain of the Silkies but also a great fiddler. All Pa said was that things were different in those days.

The only time I saw Pa dance in public was at the winter fête two years ago, when I was eleven. And the marvelous sight of Pa dancing was what got me so interested in music and led to all our trouble. A master fiddler by the name of Jubal Hatcher came to that fête, and his bow work could have matched Great-Great-Grandpa's.

Jubal Hatcher was an old friend of Pa's. They had hunted Hydra together when they were both boys. Jubal ran a resort down south in the marshlands for fishermen and fleet mechanics. During the winter when things were slack, he and his wife Poppy, a little plump partridge of a woman, came up north in their boat, playing music all around the country just for the fun of it.

And the first thing Jubal did when he came to Old Sion was to ask us for a drink of "the only cool, sweet, fresh water for a hundred miles." My family, thanks to Great-Great-Grandpa Lamech, had the only fresh water in Old Sion. The others had to catch rainwater in tanks or distill seawater in evaporating pans. In the very early years of the colony, when the sea began to rise and the colony tried to hold it back with dikes, Great-Great-Grandpa had the foresight to sink a pump down to the water table underneath the house.

Then when the other four families in the house moved

out, Great-Great-Grandpa made an imitation well after a story he had read about Earth. He disconnected the pipes to the fourth and fifth floors and then used stones and mortar to form the round walls of a well. Later generations had reinforced the floor beneath the "well" with steel beams during the dry years. It was natural for visitors like Jubal to ask for our fresh water.

Pa had me fetch a bucket of water. The bucket was made of cedar and bought special from the mainland. Jubal dipped a gourd into it and brought the gourd up to his lips while the breeze from the window gently blew his soft gray hair all around like a silver flame. His Adam's apple worked up and down as he swallowed. "Now that is perfection," he said, and gave his wife the gourd.

Then he raised his fiddle and shouted out, "Gonna play 'Sweetwater,' neighbors." It was an old hymn from Earth and Pa's favorite.

He began to tap his boot, the high heel clicking nicely on the concrete roof of the old abandoned warehouse we used for the fête. He settled the fiddle easily between chin and shoulder and he brought the bow down caressingly on the strings and began to play.

Jubal's cheek and lip kind of twitched over the fiddle and his beard jerked up and down. There was Ma nodding her head slowly so that her hair bounced about like a sea. And there was Caley trying to squirm out of Ma's arms to get closer. And there was Pa himself sitting quiet in his chair, his eyes gleaming, his hand softly slapping the table. It put him into just the right mood.

When Jubal started the next song, Pa couldn't take it

anymore, so he got up out of his chair. Pa was a big man with a solid, square face and long black hair. In his Captain's uniform he looked even stronger and more impressive. On a public occasion like the fête he usually seemed as if he were just about to be inspected by an admiral, but that night he rolled up the sleeves of his Captain's tunic so that the scars from his Hydra-hunting days showed, and he unbuttoned his collar. Then he turned to Ma with a grin.

Ma was a tall woman with a solid frame, but she could move real light and easy. And when she smiled, she could be as pretty as any girl in the Commune. She was smiling now. She did love music, though out of love for Pa she rarely let it show in public. But now she could forget about being the Captain's wife because the Captain himself had forgotten.

She let Caley slide off her lap and she stood up, gracefully brushing the wrinkles from her formal dress. She and Pa looked fifteen years younger—as fresh as they must have the day they began courting. She let Pa take her in his arms and they danced out there on the floor—No, not danced, they floated out there with hardly any effort. I got to see what Pa must have been like before he became the Captain and had to start taking life so seriously.

And I wanted that music so bad. You might call it hillbilly music and even a mainland foolishness, but that's all right; there was never any kind of music that wouldn't catch you as long as it was done right before you. Music is music, I don't care what type, be it free jazz or a child's off-key singing. It's music if it reaches inside and makes you want to keep time right along from the tapping of your toes to the nodding of your head because you want to be part of that rhythm.

After that night when I saw what music could do, there was nothing for me to do but whittle out a flute. I just had to be a musician. What with school in the morning and chores in the afternoon, I only had an hour of spare time every day before dinner, but I was determined to make the most of it. I found out that while it may be hard to listen to a beginner learning how to play an instrument, it's twice as bad to be the beginner and know that you're playing badly.

First my parents chased me out of the house, and then there did not seem to be one place in the city where I could go without some Silkie turning up to make fun of me. I got so sensitive about it that every time someone laughed, I thought they had to be cracking a joke about me. But if it was hard on me, I should have known that it was twice as hard for my Pa.

Pa was caught between being a father and being a Captain. On the one hand, he understood how I felt about music, but on the other hand, he didn't want his son to become the idiot of the Commune. Pa hinted that a Captain's son should have a little more dignity, but he didn't do anything, hoping I'd get tired of it. For five months he did not interfere while his son made a fool of himself, but finally there came a point where he lost his patience.

It was on the day in early spring that Jafer Purdy rowed up to the abandoned house I was in and howled like a Hydra. I tried to ignore him but I only made more mistakes with my fingering and breathing because I knew someone else was around. Finally I just had to get at Jafer but he was already halfway down the street and rowing like mad. By the time I got home, the story was all around the Commune. Ma didn't say anything to me about it though, and I was grateful for that.

But unfortunately it was clear that Caley also knew about Jafer. Ma must have warned her to be nice to me and not to tease me, which only annoyed me all the more. During that whole afternoon Caley did not ask me even one time to read her a story or play with her. She did not contradict me when I said anything. She did not argue with me when I gave her an order. It was kind of scary seeing Caley be so good.

It wasn't in the natural order of things for us to get along so well, and when we finally had our fight, it was a good one. It started out harmlessly enough. I had forgotten and left a chair away from the table, so that Caley bumped into it. You see, Caley moved around the house by memory alone. Usually you could hardly tell that she was blind.

You had to be careful not to notice when she bumped into something, because then she'd just laugh and slip around whatever she had stumbled against, tracing its position with her sensitive fingertips. But some of the time not noticing was not as easy as it sounded.

I put down the old book I was reading. "I'm sorry, Cal."

She turned toward me. "What's to apologize for?"

"For leaving the chair out."

"It's all right," Caley said cheerfully.

"No, it's not all right. It was stupid of me."

"Don't you baby me." Caley stamped her foot.

"Then break your old neck. See if I care."

Caley opened her mouth once or twice but couldn't find anything nasty enough to say, so she just went back to her favorite corner and flopped down, pulling her fur rug up around her legs. Then she started to stare at me.

Caley has long silver hair like Ma's and sometimes Ma puts tiny little bells on Caley's braids so that she chimes every time she moves. No matter where I went in the room, now, I could hear Caley's bells ring faintly as she turned her head to stare after me. It got so that I could just about feel her eyes following me. But on that afternoon I wasn't going to give Caley any kind of satisfaction. I picked up my book and sat down in a chair right in front of her corner and pretended to read while Ma, exasperated with the two of us, concentrated on getting dinner ready. Caley and I had an unspoken rule to make up before Pa came home. It was pretty hard not to because dinner time in the Commune is one of the nicest, most peaceful of times. You could hear the clanking of pots from all over the Commune as other mothers prepared dinner like our Ma, and you could hear the drone of voices grow louder as one by one the men returned.

But that day was different. I think both of us wanted to make up but we were both as proud and stubborn as we Priests can be, and we waited too long. When we heard Pa answer the watchman's challenge, Ma reached the balcony first, quietly smoothing the front of her smock.

I held back when Caley stirred from her corner. She walked slowly and carefully across the room with that odd, dancing grace of hers, her arms held out from her sides. She was tall for a girl of seven and very slender, so at that moment I agreed with Pa when he said that Caley looked more like an elf than a human. I wanted to apologize to her but she felt me hovering nearby and she waved impatiently at me. "Go on, I can take care of myself."

I swallowed my apology and went to the balcony.

"You'd better watch your sister," Ma said.

"She doesn't want to be watched."

"There's a big difference between what you want and what you get," Ma scolded me. "I thought you'd know that by now." And Ma stood sideways so she could see both Caley and the street, because sometimes Caley could be reckless when she wanted to prove she did not need to be "babied."

Shamefaced, I caught the mooring line of Pa's boat when he threw it up. He waited until I had tied the line to the railing and then he lifted his salvaging sack up to me. Pa liked to come home like a typhoon, sweeping everything and everyone in the house. Usually he would kiss Ma hello right away while he was still climbing over the railing of the balcony, and then he would hug Caley to his chest and swing her into the room and around in the air—with her screaming gleefully all the while.

But that day he saw all our faces and he stopped grinning. Ma gave him only a little peck and Caley shied away from him just like an elegant young cat. He heaved a big sigh and shooed us all inside, carefully closing the doors behind him. He hooked his thumbs into his belt and inspected us each in turn.

"Well now, supposing someone tells me what's wrong?"

"Wrong?" Ma asked.

Pa nodded. "I feel like the man in the story who comes home to find the Elf King's stolen his family and put some magical ones there instead. You can't tell me this is my 'real and beloved' family. All I see here are long faces."

"It's been a tiring day, Inigo." Ma moved away to start dinner.

"That I don't doubt, what with two children fighting all day." Pa looked at Caley and me significantly. "You know, Tyree, you've been getting awful hard to live with since you took up that notion to be a musician."

"Yes, sir," I mumbled.

"This isn't the first time I've come home to a strange family, but I think this is the worst day, and that wouldn't be because you and Jafer Purdy met a Hydra this afternoon, would it?" Pa tried to keep his voice sounding casual but he couldn't help letting a little angry note creep into it.

"It wasn't a Hydra," I said, turning red. "It was me."

"Well, to hear Jafer tell it, you saved his life. It seems you made a sound like the biggest, meanest Hydra afloat and scared the real Hydra away. Jafer's saying you got a magic touch when it comes to imitating Hydra sounds."

"He was just having his fun."

" 'Pears like a lot of folk have had fun with you. I would think you'd be tired of it by now. I know I am." Pa unzipped his wet suit. "I also talked to Erasmus today. He said your schoolwork was slipping."

"And why shouldn't it?" Ma asked. She placed the pot on the fireplace crane and swung it over the fire. "He's already eleven and the oldest boy there. He knows enough as it is."

"I know. I know." Pa put his hand affectionately on my shoulder and gave me a shake. "But there's got to be somebody who can read the logbooks in Anglic and understand what our forefathers said. We can't afford to lose any part of our heritage. Now can we?"

"No, sir," I said.

"So maybe it's best if you spend that extra hour on your

translation instead of on fooling around."

I looked up at him but he was as stern as ever. Ma busied herself around the fireplace, so I saw that I'd have to do my own arguing. "I want to play real bad."

Pa pressed his lips together in an angry frown, so I knew the subject was closed. "Now hear me, Tyree Priest. Personally I can live with a family that you've upset, but I won't have the Captain's son become the laughingstock of the Commune. I don't want any Silkie ever to hear you play again. Is that understood?"

I immediately saw a way of obeying Pa without having to give up my music. I thought for sure he'd think of it too, but he didn't. He just waited calmly for me to say yes, because in all my life I'd never said no to him. I felt kind of shaky at my boldness but I managed to control my voice.

"Yes," I said.

"Then go on and read, Tyree," Pa said with a smile.

Caley sat on Pa's lap and I pulled out my worn notebook and smoothed down the pages that I'd copied from the logbook last night. The logbooks contained the history of the Silkies, back to the days when my ancestors first went into space. Parts of the logs had been kept in Anglic; the other parts I translated from Intergal into Anglic for practice.

I read slowly and carefully, the old Anglic phrases and formulas rolling off my tongue, stories of expeditions, scientific equations, then my poetic composition modeled after old Anglic poems. And Pa sat patiently and proudly, though Caley was the only one who even half understood me because she was the only one who had learned a few words of Anglic— mainly by osmosis. Pa wouldn't let me read the logbook in

Intergal, the hybrid tongue that's used throughout the whole empire—even though Intergal was the only one he knew. Pa said that if Anglic was good enough for our ancestors, it was good enough for him to hear.

Just about the time my throat went dry, I finished reading about those old days. I always used to time my lessons so that they would end when Ma wanted Caley to set the table. Caley took a lot of pride in setting the table the way she had been taught and wouldn't let anyone help.

It was about all I could do to keep calm during dinner, but Pa probably figured that I was fidgety over having to give up my flute-playing. Anyway, he told me stories about the days when he was a boy—and that was something Pa rarely did, because he liked his privacy. Normally it would have been a treat, but I was so nervous that all I wanted us to do was to go to bed.

I figured that Pa's order could be taken two ways, his way and my way. I could play the flute as long as no Silkie heard me, and I knew there was one place at night in Old Sion where no Silkie would hear me, because no Silkie would dare go there. I was willing to go there that very night to find a place where I could practice. I planned to go to Sheol. I was that desperate.

We still called the area by its old name, given when Sheol was the most elegant and expensive area in Old Sion, but now after the floods the mansions were occupied by the Argans, the only intelligent race native to Harmony. The Argans were a strange race, and they liked to keep their secrets. No human ever knew how they reproduced, though their words for family relations translated loosely into "uncle" and "nephew."

There were some humans who had never forgiven the aliens because they didn't warn the colonists about the tides, but then we weren't asked to come to their world. And anyway, the colonists weren't exactly kind to the aliens.

Later when the city, Old Sion, was abandoned, the Argans drifted back from the wastelands, claiming that the land was still theirs, and by that time it did not matter who Old Sion belonged to legally, because the sea had already filled most of the city. There was a silent agreement between the humans and the Argans—though both would have been the first to deny it—not to go into certain sectors, or at least never to be seen there. No man ever saw an Argan in Old Sion unless that Argan wanted him to, not even if it was in that human's own home. So when I went into the Argans' area, I was the one in the wrong. I was the invader.

At night Sheol didn't look like it belonged to man anymore. The half-submerged elegant houses looked like ancient monsters surfacing. Their great stone faces were covered with delicate beards of green seaweed or soft mustachios of barnacles. The seaworn doors opened like the mouths of Seadragons through which the water twisted and untwisted, and the windows were like eyes, hollow and black and waiting—with ripples fanning outward as though from some creature sleeping inside.

It was really scary, but I thought like a human in those days and I figured that whether the Argans and the animals and the houses liked it or not, I was going to practice there. On purpose I picked out the finest and biggest mansion, which had been built on a hill. It had belonged to Nimrod Senaar, the Governor who had cheated my ancestors. The statue of our old enemy rose from the water lonely and proud, frowning at the change in his old city. I thumbed my nose at him as I passed.

I moored my skiff to one of the pillars of the portico and splashed up the steps. My bare feet made wet slapping sounds as I walked across the portico and through the entrance hall with its huge rotunda. I checked the rooms on both floors for the acoustics until I found one that satisfied me. Then for about an hour I practiced my scales until I heard something strange.

At first I thought it was the wind but then I realized it was music, and the more I listened, the more I felt that I had never heard anything more lovely. The song was at once sad and yet beautiful, moving like the veiled ghosts of bold knights or unfulfilled maidens. The echoes floated up the street over the hissing water, past the empty, slime-covered apartment houses, bounced and danced past walls whose rotting mortar slowly spilled stone after stone into the sea. It was a song for Old Sion.

I had to find the musician and I searched the entire mansion until I found him sitting on the portico by my skiff. It was an Argan, an old one, sitting there calmly. The bristly fur on his back and arm-legs was a peppery gray, the flesh on his belly was all wrinkled, and he stooped slightly from old age. He looked very much like a four-foot-high Earth spider, though you would never suggest that to an Argan. They hate to be reminded of their resemblance to their Earth cousins the way humans hate to be reminded that they look like apes.

He put down his reed pipes when he saw me and with six of his arm-legs slowly pushed himself off the portico. He seemed surprised and walked around me. He walked delicately on two arm-legs like a ballet dancer imitating an old man, with his six other arm-legs stretched out to balance his overpuffed body. He stepped back in front of me and examined me boldly, even though Argans usually kept their eyelids down low because they knew how their eyes bothered humans. Argans have myriads of tiny eyes on their orbs. They shine like clouds of stars in dim light and it takes some getting used to—it's like being watched by a one-man crowd.

"What can I do for you, Manchild?" he asked in Intergal.

I shifted uncomfortably from one foot to the other. I told myself that it was silly to feel like I had invaded this Argan's home. In those days I believed I had as much right to this place as the Argans did. "I heard you playing," I said finally.

"And my nephews and my neighbors heard your free concert," the old Argan said. "They found me and told me so I could come home and hear my competition."

"There's no competition," I mumbled. It was easy enough to get embarrassed about my playing in those days. I could even be shamed by aliens. "Well," I added, "I guess I'll be moving on. I don't want to drive folk away from their homes."

The old Argan grabbed hold of me and I knew I couldn't get away. The Argans had small but very strong disc-shaped suction pads at the base of their finger-toes. They could retract the suction pads into their skin or extend them so that the bottoms of their hand-feet appeared to be rimmed with tiny white circles. When he used his suction pads, his grip was unbreakable.

"What do they know? It's the song that counts, not the

singer." He pointed at the flute. "And that's a mighty nice flute. Did you carve it?"

I turned my ornate flute over in my hands self-consciously. "I'm afraid I spent more time carving pictures into it than I did playing it."

"Do you like music?"

"More than anything," I said. "But there's no one to teach me."

"Of course." The old Argan was thoughtful for a moment. "What did you think of my song? It was just a little night music."

"I thought it was beautiful," I said and added truthfully, "it was the most beautiful thing I've ever heard."

I don't know what he was looking for, but he studied me for a long time. His myriad eyes reflected my image so I saw a hundred Tyrees—each a perfect miniature.

"Would you like me to teach you?" the old Argan said.

"But what about your nephews and your neighbors?"

"I told you to forget them. Music's the only important thing."

I felt a warm rush of gratitude inside me. "I'd like it an awful lot if you would teach me, Mister . . ." I realized that I had almost made a bad mistake, because Argans, like some people on Earth, don't believe in giving their true names because that gives the listener power over the person named. Argans have what they call use-names, which they change every so often.

"My use-name is Amadeus." The old Argan let go of my wrist with a slight popping noise.

I rubbed the small circles on my wrist where the suction pads had gripped me. A new question had occurred to me but

17

it took me awhile before I worked up enough nerve to ask him. "Since you're an Argan, how can you teach me to play a human musical instrument?"

"It's enough that I know," Amadeus snapped. "Now no more questions if you want me to teach you."

It was a puzzle how an alien could teach me about human music, but I was willing to try anything. "All right," I said.

"Come back tomorrow night and I'll see if I can teach you that you have only two thumbs and not ten."

I knew that I had met one of the aliens songsmiths, and all the way home I felt warm and good inside, knowing what a privilege I was being given. If there is one thing the Argans love, it's their music—you could hear one or more of them playing on their reed pipes whenever you passed near Sheol. The Argans think that the gods directly choose someone to be a songsmith. Important councils have been moved to decisions by an inspired songsmith suddenly getting up and playing a particular song in a particular way.

The Argans don't think of music as we humans do. An Argan song seems skimpy by human standards. It just has a basic story line—like how the three moons were created—and a theme of music which represents the song. It's up to the musician to improvise and create variations on the theme and to combine these with certain other established themes which the audience recognizes as representing a castle, or a feast, or a heroic battle, or anything like that.

In Argan music, songs keep on evolving and changing as they are played. The Argans think that the human style is the mark of a mediocre musician. Only mediocre musicians play a song in the same way all the time. In human music, since you usually have a song sheet, the musician is limited to an already-fixed pattern of themes and variations and his performance is judged by his skill in playing the song. But in Argan music, the best musicians have to be not only skilled craftsmen but also geniuses at finding new and original patterns.

Of course, Argan music isn't really that loose. When I first started to play it, I wondered how a musician knew what to play next, since you had to choose while performing at the same time; but there's a kind of logic to it—like knowing the ending to a story halfway through the telling. For example, if two Argan heroes meet, you have to describe both of them, and their battle, and the funeral for the loser.

Amadeus was very patient about explaining things like that about music. He really earned his title, the Ultimate Uncle—which was his social position among the Argans, though Amadeus would never tell me any more. He hated to talk about himself and Argan affairs, but about music there was almost no stopping him. I took to visiting Sheol three times a week, and Amadeus would listen patiently as I butchered his people's music. Whenever I tried to apologize for a particularly clumsy performance, he would encourage me by telling me that my song and I had not found one another yet. According to Argan belief, it's the song that finds the singer and not the other way around.

After a while, though, not even that belief could satisfy me. I was tired from having to do my chores during the daytime, keep my secret from my parents, and still have nothing to show for all my sacrifices but some bad playing.

"It's no use, Amadeus. I'm never going to be a musician."

Amadeus sighed and shook his head. "Manchild, you have

everything that a person needs to make music: you have the talent, you have the skills now, but you still hold your soul back from the music—like you can't forget you're a human playing Argan music. You just have to remember that it's the music that counts—not the one who plays it."

And with that he put the reed pipes to his mouth and began to play the human song, "Moonspring." I sat in astonishment as he slipped next into "Shall We Gather by the Stars" and "These Happy Golden Years."

"Amadeus, where did you ever learn to play human songs?" I asked in amazement.

He made a disappointed noise. "Manchild, didn't I just tell you that a real musician can play both 'human' and 'Argan' music? I'm not an Argan playing human songs. I'm a musician making music. The only thing that matters in this changing universe is the song, the eternal song that waits for you."

"Yes, but—"

"Play," Amadeus angrily ordered me, so I played. It was strange. Amadeus wouldn't talk about himself and he wouldn't let me talk about myself; and yet despite my ignorance, I felt closer to him than I had to anyone else. And in the moments when I doubted myself, Amadeus somehow always managed to keep me looking for my song.

Anybody who thinks Argan music is easy to learn has never really tried it. A lot of it was boring work when I had to master all the conventional themes so I would have a variety to choose from; but eventually after a year's work I got so that I could play two songs tolerably well. Even Amadeus had to admit I was a tolerable backup man—though I had yet to be found by my own song. But then one night he sat for a long time and smoothed the hair down on his arms thought-fully before he finally looked up at me again. "I don't know what to do, Manchild. You're not going to develop any more unless you listen to others play—and you play for others."

Amadeus knew all about my first bad experiences with an audience, so he knew how shy I was of those situations. "Amadeus," I finally said, "have they been staying away because of me or have you been keeping them away so I wouldn't be nervous?"

"A little of both," Amadeus said reluctantly.

"The Argans don't like the idea of your giving me lessons, do they?"

"Who told you?" he asked angrily. "You pay those fools no mind. They've heard you play but they just won't believe."

"Believe what?" I asked.

"That an Argan song will ever find a human," Amadeus was forced to admit.

"Have they been giving you trouble?" I asked.

"It doesn't matter," Amadeus said.

I had noticed that the rooms were a lot dustier of late, as if most of the house was no longer occupied. A brilliant song-smith like Amadeus should have had quite a few Argans around him—not only to hear him play but also to serve him as befitted his status. Yet whenever I went over there, Amadeus was alone.

"Do your family come back after I leave, or do they stay away all the time now?"

"Mind your own business," Amadeus snapped.

"But, Amadeus—"

Amadeus held up one hand-foot as a warning. "Let's get

something straight, Manchild. We're here to play music, not to talk."

I gave up asking any more questions and just thought for a while. After all he had done for my sake I could hardly do less. "If you can get some of them together, I'll play for them," I said. "We'll show them."

Amadeus made sure I wanted to go through with it before he named the next night for my test. I had to trade twenty feet of my best nylon fishing line to Red Genteel, but he agreed to do my chores in the garden for that day while I napped. I wanted to be at my best for the Argans.

That night there must have been some twenty Argans sitting on the porch; six of them were my "classmates" while the others were nephews, skeptics, critics, and creatures who liked to see minor disasters. The moment I sat down to warm up they began to crack jokes in the clicking language of the Argans. I did not know the words but their jokes were obviously about me. They might not be able to make fun of Amadeus, but I was fair game.

One of them, Sebastian, had painfully learned some Intergal, so I could understand. "My cousin, he say, are your fingers broke? But I say, no, you just sitting on your hands."

I started to blush but Amadeus, he gave me a wink—which for an Argan is a considerable maneuver. It was a mannerism that I thought he had picked up from me. "You just start whenever you like, Manchild. Don't you mind the noise. 'Pears to be an undue number of insects out tonight." Amadeus stopped their jokes for maybe a minute and then they started in again. If I had been Amadeus, I would have been jumping up and down with anxiety, but Amadeus had a quiet kind of strength. He was like a calm pool of water that you could have dropped anything into and it wouldn't have disturbed the pool besides a momentary ripple. Just having Amadeus there gave me confidence.

"I'd like to play now, Amadeus," I said.

"Well," and Amadeus nodded to me approvingly, "well, go on."

I shut my eyes against all the furry faces and the starclustered eyes and I tilted my head up toward the night sky, toward the real stars. Suddenly my song had found me. It was "Sweetwater," the song Jubal had played at that winter fête— but now I made it my own. I took the melody and I played it like an Argan, modeling my song after an Argan song about a lost child looking for its mother. All the months of frustration and loneliness poured out of me and I played like I was the lost, lonely child calling across the empty light-years of space to Mother Earth.

The notes blended into a song that floated majestically over the rooftops, wheeling like a bird fighting through the wind and the rain, striving to break into the open, free sky, where the sun would dry his wings so he could turn toward home: to ride the winter winds to his home. I felt as lonely as when I used to lie on the roof watching the flocks of birds overhead and imagining what it was like to fly. Gliding with long, strong wings—floating along through the light, so far above the world that land and sea blurred into one. The wind raced through their pinions, bore them up on an invisible hand, and then, passing through their bodies, there came the smell of sweetwater.

When I felt the song was finished, I put the flute down to

see Amadeus chuckling to himself. The other Argans looked a little stunned. Amadeus started to play a theme, this time an Argan song, "The Enchanted Reed Pipes." I played backup man but he was the master, sending his song ringing and echoing up the abandoned streets, the two of us gone mad with music.

# 2

## THE PRICE OF A SONG

MAYBE AMADEUS HAD been trying to do no more than befriend a lonely human, or maybe he was trying to make a point to the other Argans about music in general. He might have been trying to do both; I don't know. Gradually his class got curious about my musical heritage. Sebastian especially liked the passionate human songs about suffering and death, and Handel liked the short religious hymns. At first we tried them the Argan way but using human songs, and then we tried human songs the human way of playing, and I found to my surprise that I didn't have any trouble with human songs anymore.

And the feeling grew inside me that by combining the musics of Earth and Harmony I was creating music that would belong particularly to the Silkies: songs that would celebrate all the hard times and high times of being a Silkie—yes, and maybe I was creating our soul; for it's a grand and yet a frightening thing to be a Silkie.

To be a Silkie, your ancestors must have lost the stars. For generations before they came to Harmony, my ancestors had manned the same fleet of starships. If you live on Earth, I don't have to tell you why; you already know that there isn't enough metal or good soil left on Earth to satisfy her needs. Earth could not survive if her colonies did not ship food and ore to her.

In order to set up as many colonies as possible, all the starships had been kept in service—even the old antiques. In two centuries my ancestors carried twenty-three groups of colonists from Earth to different stars. The space crews took their families with them so that their sons and daughters could replace them during the long voyages. Six generations of my ancestors grew up and died in their ships, so that the starships were their only real home. But when my ancestors finally brought the colonists to Harmony, their ancient starships could not lift off again—too many parts had worn out. There were not enough good parts in all five ships to make one ship serviceable.

There was a second fleet of ships due the next year and my ancestors expected to be taken back to Earth to be retrained and given a new fleet of modern ships. However, the Governor, Nimrod Senaar, came with the second fleet, and he refused to let my ancestors return to Earth in those ships. The Governor wanted the spacemen as technicians and engineers for the equipment he salvaged from the first fleet. Even though it might be outdated by Earth standards, there was a lot of stuff valuable to any beginning town—like computers, radios, and engines.

So to be a Silkie you must have lost the stars. And to be a Silkie you must hate the land, because it was the land which cost you the stars. Your ancestors brought the colonists here so they could work the land—ungrateful colonists who insulted and humiliated you on the land.

Great-Great-Grandpa Lamech was the Captain of the spacemen at that time and I don't think there'll ever be another man quite like him. He knew that the spacemen were helpless because the Governor had absolute authority in the colony. On principle, Earth did not interfere in its Governors' decisions, no matter how unfair.

Great-Great-Grandpa led the spacemen and their families from the ships and held them back while the colonists stripped the ships down so efficiently that all that was left of the ships were the burn marks in the soil. There were some spacemen who gave in to Nimrod out of despair and agreed to work for him, but Great-Great-Grandpa kept most of the ex-spacemen together, performing the heaviest and most backbreaking labor rather than work as the traitor, Nimrod, wanted them to work.

For the next eight years, colonists poured into Harmony so that the population in the town of Sion alone jumped from a thousand to a hundred thousand; but there was never any room on the great starships for the ex-spacemen. Ore and grain had to be shipped to Earth, and not obsolete spacemen.

They were stubborn men, who rarely used their technical and mechanical skills to help the other colonists. They lived in dormitories, keeping to themselves, and doing common labor to earn their food rations. To be honest, the ex-spacemen might have helped turn the colonists against them; but then all that was left to the spacemen after they lost their ancestral starships was a certain amount of outraged pride at being cast aside. The colonists called them fools or thought them lazy, but the spacemen counted themselves above the colonists' opinion.

To be a Silkie, then, your ancestors must have lost the stars and you must hate the land because the land and the landsmen have done you many wrongs. But above all, to be a Silkie, you must love the sea—the terrible, beautiful sea, which gives with one hand and takes with the other. On the sea you have a sense of dignity and self-respect, and the sea feeds you each day; but the sea can easily, almost casually rob you of your life and each day slowly eats away at your city until, one day, it will crumble into ruins.

It seemed a miracle when the sea rose and the dikes had to be built higher and higher each year. No one had thought to check about the cycle of tides, or about the three moons. At the beginning of the dry years, or the land years, the sea was at its lowest level because there was only one moon in the sky at any one time. Gradually though, two of the three moons would start appearing in the night sky together until at the end of fifteen years, there were always two moons out of the three in the night sky at any one moment and the sea level rose higher. At the end of ten more years, the three moons appeared together and the sea level reached its highest. These ten years were called the sea's years. Then gradually in the next twenty-five years, only two moons would appear together, and then finally only one, and the sea receded.

The ex-spacemen had kept their logbooks as faithfully on Harmony as they had when they traveled between the stars, and I've read a little about those exciting days when they were creating a Silkie life-style. The ex-spacemen had not dared to live on the open sea as sailors, since they knew as little about the sea as they knew about the land, but a city that was partly underwater was a different matter. And whether it was sea or dry land between the Silkies and New Sion, they only went there to sell some of their salvage or surplus catch of fish.

It made me love my city even more when I found I wanted to write songs about it. I wanted to hear every sound and to see everything with newer, sharper eyes. I wanted to show people what it was like to live according to some grand, slow, stately scale of time. But I found that there was no human for whom I wanted to play—not even Caley. The humiliation of playing for humans was still too strong a memory, I guess. Maybe I never would have played for humans and maybe none of the other things would have happened, either, if Pa had not salvaged the trumpet.

I had just turned thirteen last autumn when Pa brought the trumpet home. Even now I'm not sure whether to bless that night or curse it; and even if, knowing what troubles the trumpet would bring us, I could go back in time, I don't think I could destroy the trumpet.

I remember every detail of that fateful night. After supper, Pa had us gather round him as usual so he could show us what he had managed to salvage that day. Because it was cold, Pa had stoked the fire until it was good and roaring. The firelight was ruddy all around us, softening all the colors and warming the soul as well as the body.

When we were all comfortable, Pa opened the sack slowly, teasingly, until he had both Caley and Ma just about to fall off the sofa with curiosity. He took out the first thing that he'd salvaged that day, wrapped in the under-sack of damp-smelling seaweed fibers.

Pa always described each item in a way that made each new thing exciting. Only that day the pickings had been poor and Pa was trying to be funny to make up for it. You could tell he was straining himself but we tried to laugh twice as hard.

"Hey ho, missy!" Pa leaned over and arched one eyebrow at both Caley and Ma. "And what wouldn't a pretty miss give us for a song?" he sang from one of the old ballads.

And he whipped the fiber bag off the object in his hand like a magician and held up the trumpet. It was old and it had been underwater and the gold plate had just about worn off. The brass was now patinaed with green mold, but underneath in spots you could see the metal and it winked delightfully, almost begging you to send air vibrating through its body again.

"Think you can fricassee it?"

"I think that bird's been done once too often," Ma said skeptically. She took it in her hands gingerly, hesitating to give it to Caley because it was so dirty. But Caley reached over eagerly to Ma's lap.

"What is it? Do tell me, Mama."

"Very poor pickings," Pa said, suddenly getting discouraged. "Very poor pickings."

"You ought to get something from Pishtim for melting it down," Ma said.

Pa shook his head and he put his hands between his knees, his knees drawn up and bent out. "At a penny per pound, that makes all of six cents if we were lucky—and if Pishtim were drunk—and if I could put my hands on the scale . . ."

Caley was fretful today. Nothing seemed to please her; she was just looking for an excuse to go into one of those tight-lipped pouts. "I want to see. I want to see." She pulled away impatiently from Ma's hands. Sometimes she could really be exasperating. Ma gave it to her and Caley's fingers raced delicately over the surface. Caley's "seeing" wasn't our normal seeing. "It feels like cold fire."

"Let me have that, Pa," I asked, trying to keep the eagerness out of my voice.

Pa twisted his head around and grinned. " 'Tain't good to eat, Tyree."

"I'm sure, Pa," I said. It was all I could do to keep from jumping off the floor and snatching it from Caley's hands.

"Trumpets are for people to make music with, aren't they, Mama?" Caley asked.

"Well, yes, dear," Ma said sadly. "But it isn't so one-sided as that. They don't make music by themselves. Someone has to blow on them first. And the person who knows how to tickle those valves is long since five fathoms deep."

"Oh," Caley said with a sigh.

Ma added wistfully. "But it would be a pity to just melt that down, Inigo."

"I don't know." Pa glanced at me.

"Oh, what harm can it do?" Ma asked.

"You wouldn't try to play it, Tyree?"

"Not me, Pa." I was telling the truth. I knew that I could never play it—but I thought it would make a good present for Amadeus.

"Well, I still don't know." Pa shook his head slowly.

"But Tyree's been so good about the flute, Inigo, and if he can't play it, there shouldn't be any problem." I squirmed uneasily on my chair when Ma said that.

Pa looked at the trumpet in Caley's hands. "Well, Tyree *has* been understanding about the flute and all. And it would be a shame to lose a relic like that." Pa snapped his fingers. "We'll just let that old skinflint Pishtim keep his pennies, hey?"

I got up, remembering to be slow about it, and to take the trumpet gently from Caley. I held it tremblingly, afraid I would break it.

" 'Bout time to do your lessons for tomorrow," Pa said.

"The lamp's all filled with moss," Ma said. "Just take the cover off." Then she pulled me close and whispered, "And the metal polish is on my table upstairs."

I looked guiltily at Ma. She patted me reassuringly on the shoulder. "Go on, one day's lessons done half well won't do you any harm. Not a boy as smart as you. I know you won't make a habit of doing that."

"No, ma'am," I said. The stairs outside the apartment were dark and cold.

Each floor of the house only amounted to a one-room apartment. The first two floors were flooded and the third floor was used as a combination dining room, kitchen, and living room. We used the fourth floor for sleeping and the fifth floor for our workroom.

Against the north wall of the workroom was Pa's work-bench, where he used to mend and weld and remake things before he tried to sell them to the junk dealers who came out from New Sion occasionally. Ma had a sewing table against the east wall and Caley had a listening corner—where she listened to the street and the sea swallows. Our family never ate birds because Caley loved songbirds, and every spare scrap we had that did not go into the bait box went to feed her birds.

My desk was against the south wall next to the balcony, so

that if I half turned in my chair, I could look at the rest of the Commune. All the houses were the same, five-story brick tenements where the spacemen and other misfits and greenhorns had been housed. After the flood, the Silkies could have moved on to better houses, but they preferred staying.

It had been a miserable place, but with the coming of the sea, the whole street had been washed clean. Everything that had happened before was just a bad nightmare and this was the real dream, with the sky soft and indecisive in the moonlight, the rotting brick faces masked with red and yellow growths of worms, layers of life that softened the hard surfaces of the city, as if warm flesh were slowly growing on bare bones. The birds huddled for the night like fat drops of snow on the roofs, and the voices rising soft and low from a hundred throats all merged into one sound that hung still over the dark waters in the street.

I took the cap off the lamp. The moment the moss made contact with the air it began to glow. The leaves of the logbooks were crumbling in the damp air, so I had to be careful when I turned the pages. I whipped through my lessons for tomorrow so my conscience wouldn't bother me. Then I got the polish from Ma's table and I rubbed the trumpet carefully with an old rag, working steadily at the patina and the sea growths until under the patient massaging of my fingers, the trumpet began to gleam, lonely and lovely, burning golden red like the heart of a fire. I oiled the valves, testing their give. They seemed okay, though I oiled them again to be sure. With a fine file and oil I worked over the inside of the trumpet until I could see a round hole inside.

Ma must have figured that I wanted the trumpet to hang

on the wall, but I had a better use for it. It was really Caley who had given me the idea when she had wished for a musician. Whether Amadeus could play it or not, I was sure that he would treasure it.

Just as I finished polishing the trumpet, Ma called up to me that it was time to go to bed. I stored the trumpet down in my desk quickly as I heard the creaking sounds of Pa's footsteps on the stairs. I thanked Ma secretly in my heart for the warning. Pa had come up to tell me to fetch more wood for the fourth-floor fireplace so he could start the fire. Caley liked to have a fire going in the sleeping room when she told her story.

Sometimes when I was younger I used to close my eyes and try to imagine what it must be like not to see, but all I wound up doing was getting lost in the dark and bumping into things, so that Ma had to tell me to stop. Anyway, I don't see half the things with both eyes that sightless Caley sees. Not just her trolls and golden-haired princesses, but the details, the cigarette tip pulsing like a star in the dark night or the pattern of waves sweeping along the shore—things that we have remarked on casually for her and that she has retained in her encyclopedic memory.

She speaks of ancient wars on Earth, of creatures of light and things of darkness. She tells us about our ancestors, not as they were but as they should have been. And you listen enthralled to the skinny little girl, kneeling with her back to the fireplace, almost breathless from the words she is continuously throwing out.

"There was a musician," Caley began, "who charmed stars out of the sky to dance around his legs. And the kings and queens, knights and princesses, Helens and Hectors, even a demon or two, would gather from miles around to hear him play, until the field would be glittering with gemmed, robed, beautiful people dancing to his tunes."

She went on to tell how that musician once saved a kingdom which was being destroyed by a huge giant. The musician played such fantastic music that the giant could not stop dancing. He danced for a solid week until he had stomped a hole a mile deep, and then—and only then—did he fall asleep on his feet. The musician leaped downward, landed on the giant's back, and cut off the giant's head.

Then the musician found that he could not climb out, so he put the head on one foot and sat down on the other foot and played such music that the trees started tapping their roots and the mountains swayed, and the dead, well, the dead started to rise, or at least to kick. The musician played polkas and cancans and every lively tune he knew until the giant's body started to pound its fists and kick its feet in time to the music. The musician played till his lips were sore and his cheeks were tired. Whole forests did the square dance and the mountains did hornpipes and the giant's body gave a one-two-three kick that sent the musician and the head both sailing out of the hole and onto the surface again. And the musician returned home with a huge bag of gold so he did not have to play for a year and his mouth and cheeks could recover.

When Caley had finished, she sat back with a sigh. "I wish," Caley said, "I wish we could have music." And I had to agree with her. We *ought* to have had music proper to that dream city.

"We could sing again, Minnow, if you like," Pa said.

"Not that kind of music." Caley shook her head firmly. "I want star-charming music, music to make princes and kings and queens dance by."

"That's long gone, Caley," Ma said sadly. "I don't even know if there was ever such music."

"There must be," Caley insisted stubbornly. We might have had an argument, but Ma had us hurry up and unroll our mats and blankets and go to sleep by the fireplace. I listened until I counted one, two, three persons breathing softly and evenly. I forced myself to draw the blanket down quietly, letting the warm air slip over my body. I fetched the trumpet and I went downstairs to the third floor and out onto the balcony. The whole street was dark now except for the watchmen's lanterns at either end of the street.

I never heard Caley come down the steps. In familiar surroundings, she could move as quietly as a cat. "Tyree?" she called softly.

"Here I am, Caley," I said, taking her arm. She ran her other hand reassuringly up my arm.

"Where are you going?" Caley asked, her blanket pulled tight about her neck and the ends trailing about her. She had ears that were way too sharp.

"None of your business," I said.

"Your bedding's hardly warm in the morning, like you just climbed in and out again before I roll it up. Where are you going?"

I said carefully, "If you don't watch out, you're going to fall right into the water." It was a mean thing to say and right away I could feel my cheeks burning, because Caley hated to be told that, but it was the fastest way of getting rid of her.

She stamped her foot in annoyance. "You, Tyree."

For a moment I thought that she was going to yell at me and then everything would be all up with me. But she was so mad that she could not think of anything to say, so she just shook her head and pulled her blanket tighter about her neck and went back into the house. With a sigh, I clambered down the rope ladder into my skiff. I slipped my oars quietly into the water till I was past the men standing night watch on the roofs, but I had no more than cleared the Commune when I heard someone hiss.

"Hey, Tyree."

I almost jumped out of the boat at first, I was so scared. I turned around in my skiff to see Jafer Purdy standing on the window ledge of an abandoned house, grinning from ear to ear in the moonlight. In one hand he held a fishing line. There were a dozen floats bobbing up and down in the water and lines leading from the floats into the house.

Red Genteel elbowed his way past Jafer. "Knew you would come out tonight. I said there ain't nothing can keep Tyree from the fish and the fish from Tyree."

"Tyree?" Jara Genteel stood on tiptoe and looked over her brother's shoulder. "It's about time, Tyree."

"Who else is with you?" I asked. I turned the skiff around and kept rowing against the current to keep myself before the window.

"The whole gang, Tyree." Joktan Aesir poked his head out from another window of the building, and with him were his twin sister, Fenya, and Irad Kahn. Irad was the oldest, at fifteen. He was the eldest son of the Kahn family who grew the Commune's fresh vegetables in their rooftop gardens. Irad was a giant like his father, slow of movement and of thought, but dependable. Joktan, Fenya, Red, and Jafer were the same age as me. Jara Genteel was twelve and small, with red hair cropped short about her neck. We'd played together, fought together, hunted together, even suffered through school together, and at one time I had counted them as my brothers and sisters.

We used to go off on midnight adventures like tonight's— sometimes to fish, sometimes to visit the old spaceport—with hardly a thought to how dangerous it was. A Silkie grows up using a spear and knife. As long as you were in a group, and were sensible, like not going deliberately into a street where you knew the Hydra hunted, you were pretty safe.

"Well, with all of you out, there won't be any fish left for me to catch." I pushed off from the building with my oar.

"Now that we got you, think we're going to let you go so easy?" Fenya held out her spear. Her spearhead had a guard which kept anything she speared from pushing onto the shaft. The ends of the guard curved back so that she could use it like a boat hook. She and Joktan held onto the pole while they tried to hook the bow of my boat, but I parried every thrust with an oar until the current took me out of range. Jafer jumped into the water and made as if to hold my skiff back.

A joke was a joke but I had more important things to do that night. "Let go, Jafer," I told him and when Jafer flashed a grin at me, I held up an oar as if to knock his hands away. "I said to let go."

"What's gotten into you lately, Tyree?" he asked. He looked hurt and confused but he let go.

Red stood up on the ledge and looked into the skiff.

"He's got himself a mysterious bundle there."

Joktan snapped his fingers. "Gonna tootle your flute?"

Even though I was an adequate musician now, I was still touchy about my past failures. "You might say that," I said cautiously.

"So it's you that's kept me up every night?" Jafer asked with a grin. "All this time I been blaming the Hydra for howling." They all laughed at that and all I could do was stay silent. When Fenya saw that I was not laughing, though, she made the others hush.

"Come on, Tyree. You can give up practice one night. Come on and fish with us," she said.

"I can't, Fenya."

"Oh, let him go, Fenya. That boy needs practice if anyone ever did," Jafer said, and I could see from his eyes that if I let him, he would spread our meeting through the whole Commune tomorrow.

"Jafer and all of you, I wouldn't tell anybody else about tonight unless you want to be knocked into the street."

"I think he means it, Jafer," Red said quietly. He came to the ledge and gave Jafer a hand getting up. They all looked at me thoughtful-like and maybe a little afraid too, like they were suddenly seeing a stranger. Well, I guess I was. I mean, I'd much rather have lost their friendship than have had that story put around the Commune.

"You just remember what I said." I looked down so I wouldn't have to see their faces. "You just remember."

"All right for you, Tyree," Red said angrily. I made the oars fly then, taking out all my frustration on rowing and trying to blink back the tears. It wasn't easy trying to play my music.

By now the Argans had grown used to the sight of me, though they never said hello but went about their business as if I did not exist, which was the best I could hope for. Amadeus was waiting impatiently when I rowed up to his house.

"Where's your flute?" he demanded.

"I forgot," I said, slapping my forehead.

"What?" he said in annoyance. He came down the step perilously close to the water. Argans hated getting wet, but his finger-toes were even touching the water.

"I was too busy getting this for you."

And I undid the sack. The moonlight winked and smiled over the saucy trumpet mouth.

"Lord God almighty and all the heavenly host," Amadeus said. His plump body plopped down hard on the rock. He didn't do anything but stare at the trumpet. He sat there so quiet and so still, you wouldn't even have thought he was breathing.

"What that?" Sebastian asked.

Amadeus lifted it reverently from my hands and held it where Sebastian could see it better. "This, my boy, is aural sunshine. It takes the soul and amplifies it a thousandfold, polishes rough edges, purges, purifies, and generally cleanses the soul until it is finer and more transparent than air. There is nothing this side of paradise that can match it for tone and clarity; an angel's voice, the only instrument that angels use. And God, if there is one, would have to speak in the same tones as this."

"It's a trumpet, Sebastian," I said to him, while Amadeus went over the valves.

"Why not say so in first place," Sebastian grumbled, and

sat back down on the portico.

"Everything seems to work okay. Do you think you can learn how to play it?" I asked.

"Manchild," Amadeus said exuberantly, "there isn't any instrument around that I can't make sit up and beg for me to play it."

I started to ask him who had taught him to play a trumpet. But a look from him warned me not to ask. I watched as he put the trumpet to his lips slowly, and he let his breath slip out and his finger-toes fall one, two, three, four, on each of the valves and again up the scale.

Amadeus had a love of theatrics. He half rose off the ground, the fur bristling on his chest, his soft underside slowly expanding wetly, glistening, as he just kept on sucking in air until you wondered how there was any air left for you to breathe.

His cheeks bulged out, almost twice the size of a human's, so that his head looked as big and globular as a black, furry moon. He shut his eyes so tight they were lost in his face. The trumpet wailed a long, lost note. His breathing turned to magic, pulsing through the world. He straightened his double-jointed arm-legs with a snap and the music was like a sigh, like a breeze moving out over the restless water.

The Argans were making snuffling noises that I had never heard before from them.

Finally Amadeus plopped down on the marble again, tired out. His cheeks slowly went back to their normal shape as he sighed. And all the Argans around put down their reed pipes and patted the walls and floor with all eight hand-feet. And the moon and the stars were still there in the sky, to my surprise.

Amadeus held up a pair of his hand-feet and waved for the applause to stop. "How much?" Amadeus said to me.

"It's a gift, Amadeus," I said.

"But there's not another one like it in Sheol," Amadeus said. His unblinking, jeweled eyes looked at me so solemnly that I began to feel embarrassed. For some reason Amadeus was just as embarrassed as I was. He kept turning the trumpet over and over through six of his hand-feet. "No other song-smith has its equal."

I saw that I was touching some fine point of Argan etiquette, though I wasn't sure what it was. Instead of finding out, I tried to ignore it and wound up insulting everyone. "Quit making so much of it, Amadeus. There's plenty of those on the mainland."

Just about every hair on Amadeus stiffened and I turned to see that the rest of the class were all abristle too. It was dead silent on the portico with those swarms of eyes staring at me. When I called one of their treasures a common thing, they thought I was saying the Argans were inferior.

I took the silence as long as I could. "Amadeus, remember what you said about music being the only important thing?"

"There are other things that are as important as music," Amadeus said carefully.

"You will see," Sebastian said angrily. "We will find a treasure like no human has."

Anger has a way of infecting everyone else. I shoved myself up from the portico. "Do you think I care about that?"

Amadeus looked up at me even more sadly because I did not understand.

"I am the Ultimate Uncle," he said. "I have to pay my debts, Manchild."

"But Amadeus—"

"You'd best leave, Manchild."

I went home to bed feeling sorry for myself. It seemed like I had a talent for chasing away everyone who was close to me. I kept wondering what was wrong with me and I fell asleep to those miserable thoughts.

# 3

## THE SONS OF LIGHT

CALEY WAS NOT speaking to me the next morning, so she got into trouble with Ma because Ma could not understand why Caley was being so sullen with me. It was cowardly of me not to say anything, but I knew it would mean having to tell the whole story, and I was not about to give up my sessions with Amadeus. Luckily for Caley, Ma had no sooner begun her scolding than the Seadragon drowned her out.

A Seadragon measures nearly a half mile from her nose to the tip of her tail. Her body is sausage-shaped and weighs a hundred tons, and her powerful fins let her swim along sluggishly. She has a large triangular head rising from a long, thin, snakelike neck. Fortunately for us, the Seadragon is basically a vegetarian and feeds off the giant bull kelp a hundred miles down the coast. Normally she stayed far away from us.

There were a lot worse things than the Seadragon—like the clouds of skitters you got in the summer that bit anything that moved, or the Medusa, translucent, flowerlike animals with stinging cells that you could hardly see till they were almost on top of you, or the Hydra, squidlike animals that were faster, meaner, and hungrier than their Earth counterparts. But it was easy to forget just how harmless the Seadragon really was when she let out her bellow right next to the city.

In all of Old Sion there was no way of escaping that commanding voice. The melancholy cry moved over the water, a low moaning sound that set the stone walls to vibrating as if the houses were frightened. It felt like more than the voice of an animal: it was the voice of the sea that brick by brick was crushing Old Sion.

Pa motioned for us all to stay put while he and Shadrach Lawson went to investigate. It was hard to feel so helpless. I stood on the balcony trying to catch a sight of the Seadragon and thought I saw her head far away on the horizon, but I couldn't be sure. Ma had to spend most of her time trying to soothe Caley by holding her. The deafening noise made it all the worse for Caley, who not only could not see but temporarily could not hear us.

When the bellowing stopped a couple of hours later, the Commune stayed quiet for a long time afterward, like it was afraid talking might start the Seadragon bellowing again. Then we heard a quick babble of voices down the street asking Pa what had happened, but Pa would only say that everything was all right and not to worry.

"What was it?" Ma asked when Pa climbed into the apartment.

"The dangedest thing I ever saw, Jerusha." Pa shook his head. "There were Argans teasing the Seadragon—looked like they were playing tag or something."

"Teasing?" Ma asked.

"They kept throwing rocks at the Seadragon—couldn't have been more than a tap to the Seadragon, but it was enough. The Seadragon'd rear back and try to smash the Argan with her head and that Argan, he'd wait till the last moment before he'd jump and the others would commence teasing the Seadragon."

"Whatever for?" Ma asked.

"I think they wanted to distract the Seadragon," Pa said. "Because we no sooner saw this flash of light—like something shiny reflecting the sun—than the Argans all left and the Seadragon went back out to sea."

"Well, what could have gotten into the Argans?" Ma wondered.

"I don't know," Pa said, "but those Argans've riled the Commune worse than they ever did the Seadragon. Half the Commune wants to kill the Seadragon—even though our shotguns are like popguns to her; and the other half of the Commune wants to pack up and move to the mainland."

"Oh, Inigo, are you going to have to be gone all day talking?"

"I'm afraid so, Jerusha," Pa said. "And part of the night too, by the looks of things. So will you. You'll have to talk to the womenfolk." He turned and motioned to me.

"Sir?" I had kept myself as small and quiet as I could after Pa had mentioned the Argans.

"I want you to check the logbooks for any mention of Seadragons or of the Argans teasing anything—it doesn't just have to be Seadragons. I want to see if they do that out of habit or if this was special."

"I think it was special, Pa."

"Um, well, best check." There was shouting from outside

and Pa went to the balcony. He frowned. "Dang it. The Gribbles are trying to take Lawson's boat."

"But whatever for?" Ma asked.

"It's the biggest boat in the Commune. I imagine they want it for moving." Pa slipped a leg over the railing of the balcony. "We better get there before they start fighting."

"But Inigo, aren't we going to eat anything?"

"No time, Jerusha," Pa shouted as he climbed down the ladder. There wasn't anything Ma could do except follow Pa.

There was an awful lot in the logbooks that I hadn't read, and I didn't like to read much about our first few years on Harmony, since they're awful sad. I'd rather have read about how we took over Old Sion, but Pa had said to check for all references, so I flipped through all the logbooks dealing with our stay on Harmony. I didn't really do more than skim each selection just to see if it was what Pa wanted, and even then it took me four hours.

The moment I leaned back to stretch, Caley insisted that I read the logbooks out loud this time.

"What do you want me to read about, Caley?"

"I want to hear about Great-Great-Grandpa," Caley said. She liked to hear about Great-Great-Grandpa Lamech. The Silkies still refer to him as *the* Captain, and I think it was the memory of Great-Great-Grandpa that made Pa try so hard to be a good Captain. You could tell Great-Great-Grandpa Lamech was a vigorous man just from the bold, cursive script he used in the logbooks. Anyway, I had run across one reference to Great-Great-Grandpa and an old Argan that made me curious.

"Want to hear something new?"

"Oh, yes." And Caley settled down by my table, her head against my leg.

I picked up the correct logbook and turned the old brittle pages carefully until I found the account of the spacemen's first days on Harmony. I leaned forward slightly and squinted because the ink had faded to almost the same brown color as the pages.

*1.27.2756. Earth Standard. Worked in that miserable town for the colonists today to get our dole of food, because I want to save our supplies and because I don't want us to get soft. We work just as hard as the colonists but they treat us like poor relations come to sponge. Can't wait to get out of here.*

*I was mixing mortar for the bricklayers when I looked up and saw some aliens staring at me. I tried to outstare them. They won. Tried to go back to mixing. I told myself they wouldn't bother me. They were just curious aliens that had been drifting in and out of camp since we began building the town. Usually they look for a few minutes and leave. I looked up an hour later; they were still there. Went to lunch. They followed me. Went back to work. They followed me again. I changed places with Lawson, who was digging ditches, and they followed me. Finally got on my nerves so I asked them what they wanted. No response. Figured they didn't know Intergal so I tried to chase them away, but they moved faster than I could—even the old one; and the old one must be very old if you can judge from the gray of his fur and his wrinkles. He came back when I stopped chasing him and asked in bad Intergal, "Make music?"*

*I stared at him for a while but he seemed to be serious, so since I never turn down an audience, human or nonhuman, I sang. The aliens gave a reasonable facsimile of applause, showing good taste. The start of a beautiful friendship.*

I couldn't help thinking to myself that it was too bad Great-Great-Grandpa's fiddle got lost in the course of time. Anyway, the aliens came by every day for a month to listen to Great-Great-Grandpa, and they even managed to pick up some more Intergal to understand the songs.

Now if there was one thing Great-Great-Grandpa loved as much as singing, that was eating, so he'd combine the two and hold a clambake on the beach. The spacemen, being used to aliens of all kinds, invited the Argans to come to these evening fêtes. As a matter of fact the spacemen had more in common with the aliens than with the colonists, who as a rule stayed away from the spacemen. However, there were a few good colonists—mainly men and women who liked music and liked to play with the spacemen.

Great-Great-Grandpa and the other musicians taught the aliens how to play various human instruments, from the fiddle and guitar to the trumpet and the flute, until Great-Great-Grandpa said that if they could have found a way of making the colonists wear blindfolds, they could have passed off the Argans as human virtuosos and made a fortune by giving concerts.

But then Nimrod Senaar came and things got bad for the spacemen. All the Silkies will admit that if it hadn't been for the Argans, no one knows what the spacemen would have done. The Argans are skittish about water, but they do know how to fish and what seaweeds are edible and such. They laid the basis for the independence and survival of the spacemen on Harmony by teaching them how to live off the seashore. The Argans helped create the Silkies. By day there was hard work, but by night there was some soul-stirring music. But all good things have to come to an end.

*12.5.2758. E.S. I've never been so ashamed of my own kind. I thought something was wrong when the colonists asked the old alien to join in the concert, because the invitation didn't come from the musical colonists but from a bunch whose taste in music up to now had only been for drinking songs. The old alien borrowed my guitar and said simply that he'd pay his debts to mankind. We did not go to the concert because we knew we were not welcome in the camp; Nimrod Senaar has made that clear. But one of the colonists—the one I'd borrowed a trumpet from—came running over to get me. I went, taking along some of the Commune, and found this big tent set up with a huge sign over it saying Freak Show. At first the colonists at the tent opening didn't want to let us in, but we pushed our way past them and found the old alien on stage with a singing pig and a dog who could bark to ten. He was gamely trying to play the music we'd taught him.*

*You can bet we got him out of that tent but fast, though we had to bust all the chairs, a few heads, and my guitar in the process. Outside by the ships, I tried to apologize to him, but he stopped me. I've never seen anyone look so sad and confused. He asked me why they had done it and I could not answer him. He thanked me solemnly for all I had done, and apologized to me! To me! For being such a fool as not to listen to me and for embarrassing me, his teacher, in that way. He'd pay me back somehow. Then he left.*

*The Commune and I are agreed we'll have as little to do with the colonists as possible.*

*12.6.2758. E.S. Nimrod calls us troublemakers. No sign of the aliens.*

*12.8.2758. E.S. Nimrod Senaar wants to evict us. Maybe it's just as well. The aliens have shown me that we can live on Harmony somehow, some way.*

*Still no sign of the aliens. Must be gone for good.*


Great-Great-Grandpa had even very carefully crossed out the aliens' use-names—because of their humiliation, I suppose.

I looked up from the page for a moment. It was possible that the Argans last night had been remembering old wrongs done to them by the Mainlanders; and then for a moment I had the wild thought that Amadeus might even be the old Argan, though that incident happened a hundred and twenty-three years ago. Then I told myself that it really didn't matter, because Amadeus was my friend. Amadeus was as touchy about Argan matters as about himself, so it was no use asking. It was just another mystery about Amadeus that I would have to accept.

"Why'd you stop, Tyree?" Caley asked.

"Can't I take a breath?"

"You can breathe later. Go on." Caley gave me a poke in the ribs. With a sigh, I went on reading about how Great-Great-Grandpa finally led the spacemen away from the ships. I skipped to the good part where Great-Great-Grandpa was vindicated and the Silkies took over Old Sion, making it their own. Caley told me to end the reading there where it was happy.

It's hard to keep a secret from Caley—mainly because she

insists on knowing everything that goes on. I knew she was waiting for me to try and sneak out at night again, so I figured it wiser to wait a week. Besides, I figured a week would let the Argans' tempers cool down some. Then, too, I would have to do more of Pa's work because Pa would have to spend most of the next week trying to talk sense into a group of Silkies who called themselves the Sons of Light. The Argans' run-in with the Seadragon had stirred them up.

The Sons of Light were convinced that they needed protection—as if a giant Seadragon could surprise anyone. Now they started riding shotgun on salvaging and fishing parties until the groups grew so large that not even the dumbest fish would come out with all those boats overhead. They started coming back with smaller and smaller catches and they blamed *that* on the Seadragon!

The Sons of Light foolishness had started as far back as Great-Great-Grandpa Lamech's time. There were still some Silkies even then who could not see human "progress" as a lot of nonsense. They formed a committee called the Sons of Light, whose sole purpose was to restore electricity to Old Sion. They searched over the entire city until they found a generator. All the wire had been stripped away from the generator for the copper, but by long, determined hunts they managed to salvage enough wire from the city.

For one glorious hour the Sons of Light had their civilized light, using salvaged bulbs which ranged from streetlamp bulbs to tiny little kitchen lights from refrigerators. It must have been funny and also kind of sad to see all those families grouped around old rusting refrigerators watching the light. Then the snails and worms came through the open doors, seeking the light. The Sons of Light tried shutting their doors, but the worms and snails came through cracks in the walls or underneath the doors.

The generator was sold to a small town on the mainland, along with the wires and bulbs. Though the original project had been abandoned, the Sons of Light stayed together on one street, Alva Street, encouraging one another with one crackpot idea after another. They had never been content with the sea and inevitably trusted in gadgets more than in themselves.

Up to that week, Ma and Pa had always said we should feel sorry for them because they had the hearts of Mainlanders with the minds of Silkies. By that Pa meant that Silkie knowledge and skills were not meant to satisfy mainland desires. The life of a Silkie didn't fit everyone as well as it fitted Pa. In fact a lot of folks would have starved if it had not been for the communal sharing of food.

To a Silkie like Pa the Seadragon did not seem to be much of a problem, though Pa ignored the fact that even the wake of a passing Seadragon is enough to overturn a boat and drown a crew. Maybe you can say he wasn't a good Captain because he wouldn't recognize things like that. I don't know; but I'm Silkie enough so that my heart's with Pa even though my mind might disagree.

I have to admit that the Sons of Light tried to stay in the Commune, but as far as progress was concerned, there was only one way for Pa—the old way that was recorded in the logbooks of all the Captains before him. They had grumbled before, but after the Seadragon's visit, the heads of the Sons of Light came by every evening to argue with Pa about the need for modern safeguards. Big Ham Dudum was a short, excitable man, descended, as Pa said, from a long line of flutterbudgets and bullies; but the other man, Theophilus Gribble, or "File," was a tall lean man who would have made a good Silkie if his mainland mother had not spoiled him with her talk of "progress."

Finally one evening the Sons of Light came one last time to tell Pa that they were quitting.

"We come by to tell you the news, Inigo," File said to Pa.

"What news, File?"

"We just made a deal where we're going to get guns, air-cars, and brand-new houses."

Pa didn't hardly move. He didn't hardly breathe. "They'll be a great help with the fish run, I'm sure."

File shifted on the edge of his chair. "The Sons of Light won't be able to take part in the fish run. We took on jobs."

"What kind of jobs?" Pa asked. "Who'd pay you all that?"

Dudum chuckled. "We hired on with Fuller Satin."

"I know about the man," Pa said sternly. It was hard not to hear about one of the richest men in a hundred light-years. His father had made a fortune exploiting the older colonies and converting them into pleasure worlds where other people went for vacations. His son, Fuller Satin II, purposely picked out colonies like Harmony where the colonists would do almost anything to recapture their old prosperity—even if it meant signing away their land so folk from as far away as a thousand light-years could enjoy our sun on our beaches. He'd already ruined most of the east coast of the mainland. "I'd sooner sign a pact with the devil," Pa said.

"We're just going to take the tourists on hunting trips,

Inigo," File said defensively.

"Tour guides?" Pa said. "You've signed on with Satin to be tour guides?"

"Who cares?" Dudum shrugged. "If someone wants to pay to look at this miserable dump, what do we care so long as we get paid?"

"I don't notice you starving, Dudum," Pa said, because when Dudum sat down his potbelly seemed to get even larger and just sag there on his lap. Dudum was a notoriously bad hunter and practically had to live off the charity of the other Silkies. "It's up to you what you do to provide for the winter."

File seemed very uncomfortable when he realized that Pa did not share his enthusiasm. He looked like the man who has the unpleasant task of telling the family that a loved one has just died. "When I said 'we,' Inigo, I meant about half the Commune."

"And what do you expect the rest of us to do for the winter?" Ma asked. "We depend on the fish run for most of our food. It's hard enough to fish with the *full* Commune. What are we supposed to do? Eat bullets?"

"Easy, Mama," Pa said.

"Well, don't these worms feel any obligation to the rest of us?" Ma demanded.

"Now see here, Jerusha. We're going to chase that old Seadragon away and keep her away. And you'll be able to let Caley swim in the street without worrying about some stray water snake or Hydra biting her, because we're gonna chase all the vermin out of Old Sion." Dudum would have gone on, but File waved him silent.

Then File held his hands out pleadingly. "Jerusha, Inigo,

wouldn't you like to have electricity? None of this light moss. No more having to salt down your fish catches, because you'll have refrigerators. No more aching backs and arms from rowing all day, because you'll actually have aircars. You'll have modern doctors, modern—"

"I see," Pa said and pushed himself back from the table. Then he stood up slowly, and it didn't seem like Pa would ever finish getting up, because he just seemed to tower over everyone else in the room. He looked down at Dudum sternly and his look said more than his words. "I see that a lot of little hysterical people have convinced themselves that some animal who has never done them any harm—"

"You'll speak differently when she tries to climb into your bed," Dudum snapped.

"The Seadragon is less likely to try than your Mr. Satin," Pa said. Pa put one hand underneath Dudum's arm and lifted him half out of the chair before Dudum got the idea and stood on his own. "Thank you." Pa bowed to Dudum and then nodded courteously to File at the door. "Now, since I've had a hard day and since I expect to have an even harder day tomorrow getting ready for the fish run, I'll thank you to leave."

"But you'll only have half the Commune," Dudum protested.

Pa steered Dudum politely to the balcony. "You've gotta have someone to be picturesque for the tourists, now, don't you?" And he practically lifted Dudum over the railing and onto the rope ladder.

"We were just trying to be kind," File said as he pushed past Pa. "Think about it some, Inigo."

Pa had an unreadable expression on his face when he came

back into the room. We were all too afraid to move, let alone speak to Pa, but Caley couldn't see Pa's face and his silence scared her.

"Papa, what are we going to do?" Caley asked. She came out of her corner, walking slowly forward until Ma's hand pulled her against Ma's chair.

Pa did not answer. He just started to coil some rope roughly around his bent arm, the top of the loop caught in his hand, the bottom of the loop about his elbow. He did not turn when he spoke. "Jerusha, I'd take it kindly if you sang something."

Pa jerked the rope over his arm awfully fast so that Ma must have been worried about burns. She let her hand travel across the table toward Pa.

"What would you like, Inigo?"

"Anything. Just so long as it doesn't remind me of File."

Ma sang what Pa always liked to hear when he was mad, a nice song that Jubal Hatcher had taught us. It was a light airy tune that Jubal used when he went traveling. He called it his Poppy song because he played it himself whenever he got his wife mad at him. Ma has this beautiful, sweet voice, so pure and so high it does not seem like it could come from a human throat; and it's just perfect for this song:

"Tripping through the high grass,
   Slipping through the low grass—
   Won't you do a jig? do a reel? do a round?"

Pa went on working but his hands slowed down to a normal pace and he did not tug so hard at the rope. He let out

58

his breath all in one long sigh and turned around with a smile. I gave Caley a touch on her arm to let her know that Pa was okay now.

There came a call from the street and Pa took the lantern out on the balcony. "Hello, Tubal. What can I do for you?"

"Just came by to pay my respects," Tubal Kahn called back up.

Ma declared, "Don't we get a moment's peace?" But Ma knew very well that Tubal was one of the ones who wouldn't leave, and she got up and put an extra cup of Kavo out for him.

Pa took the basket from him as Tubal pulled himself up over the ladder and over the railing.

Tubal was a giant of a man—we called him the Green Man. He had long, kinky gray hair which he tied into a knot at the back of his head, and a patriarchal beard that spilled over his chest. He was quiet, just like his plants that he and his family loved to tend. He reminded you of a huge oak tree, with dirt always rimming his nails and earth that he could never get out of the cracks of his fingers no matter how often or hard he scrubbed them. He took off his hat to Ma and Caley and then flipped the lid up from the basket so that the light shone all around the room. "I figure since some of the folk are counting on electric lights, there ain't much use my saving all this moss."

Tubal took handfuls of the luminescent moss and piled it on the table so that the whole room was filled with a heady, pungent, dark smell. "One out of every two fools got to have electricity. Got to have water pipes and wires and the like," he said contemptuously. "Got to be just like Mainlanders."

Ma had got out a can to put some moss in but she stopped when she saw the pile on the table. "My land, Tubal. That's a year's supply there."

"Two years'," Tubal grudged. "I raise the finest light moss in the world. Burn it all night if you like, light up your whole house, light up every dang room in the city."

"But we don't have anything nearly so fine to trade with you," Pa said.

"It don't matter." Tubal shrugged. "The Sons of Light want us to tear down the greenhouses. They're eyesores, they say."

"But your grandpa built that shack during the first floods," Ma said. "How can it be an eyesore?"

"The Sons of Light," Pa said, "are more interested in aesthetic truth than in history."

We were all silent at that, because for the longest time the Kahns had been farming their greenhouses and the gardens in the city—greenhouses built laboriously on roofs out of scraps of wood and glass until they were strange, beautiful collages of Old Sion. I used to like to float by their street just to smell the sweet, green scents.

"They told me they laid claim to my house," Tubal added.

"But your family's been there for three generations," Ma protested.

"You never filed on it, did you, Tubal?" Pa said.

"No. Did you file on yours?"

"No. Who wanted it?"

"But if Tubal has to move, where will folks get fresh vegetables?" Ma protested.

"From Mr. Satin, the way he intended," Pa said.

"What if Mr. Satin doesn't like you?" Caley asked.

"That, Caley, is something I have been trying to make Gribble and the Sons of Light answer for the last two weeks." Pa set his cup down quietly, forcing himself to smile. "So what will you do, Tubal?"

Tubal watched Ma put the moss into canisters filled with nutrient solution so they would live and keep their luminescence until we needed them.

"Stay here till they chase me out, I guess." Tubal looked sharply at Pa. "What will you do, Captain?"

Pa gave a little smile. "Stay on."

Tubal sighed. "Maybe we're just outdated."

"To want change to come with dignity? No." Pa shook his head. Tubal got up then and the big farmer seemed to fill the whole room. He picked up his hat and spoke shyly.

"You've always a place with us, Inigo Priest."

So that was what Tubal had been trying to get at during his visit but had been too shy to bring up directly. Pa straightened up some at that, looking a little like his old self.

"I'll keep it in mind, Tubal."

Tubal started to leave and then stopped. "Oh, Tyree, my boy says hey."

"Would you please tell him hey for me too, Mr. Kahn?" I asked. It made me feel warm to know that Irad wanted to make up.

Lots of other folk came by to say the same thing. Ma was kept busy the whole evening making Kavo and washing cups. They would come in to sit for a while in the guest chairs and talk, though it seemed as embarrassing for them to talk about what had happened as it did for Pa. They would gulp down their Kavo nervously and then leave. A minute later, as if there were some prearranged order, the next group would come in. It was tiring, but it made us feel pretty good.

It was late in the evening by the time the last Silkie left. Caley had curled up in her corner, and Ma was washing the cups and dishes.

Pa looked around then at me.

"Tyree."

"Sir?"

"I figure that including the old folks and the children, we'll have about a hundred and twenty. But that means the older children will have to man the gates."

"Does that mean we're staying?" Ma asked.

"Well, I don't expect the Sunfish to come to us if we migrate," Pa said. "I'll be damned if I'll let Ham Dudum force me to give up something just because he says so."

"But using the children, Inigo?" Ma asked.

"We all have to do what we can." Pa nodded to me. "Come on and I'll show you the place where we'll set up the new run."

"But it's so late, Inigo," Ma said.

"We won't talk so long that he'll miss much more sleep than he already has." Pa pushed his chair back.

But when we got to the roof Pa just leaned over the parapet for a long time, looking first at the vast and ghostly city and then up at the full sweep of stars, the cold, distant, lonely stars. For a moment I thought the stars were the eyes of all our ancestors as they waited to see what we would do at this new point in Silkie history.

"Too few," Pa murmured. "There'll still be too few people on the gates." And suddenly I understood how he felt—

that even if he only had half a Commune, his responsibilities were as heavy as if he had a full one, maybe even heavier; but that was no reason to quit. Pa sighed. "Sorry, Tyree. If I had had my way, you would have grown up with all the time you needed to learn the city's ways, just like I had; but the world won't let us."

"Sir, I don't mind the work."

"Then we'll hold on to the city, boy. We'll manage." Pa put his arm around me and waved his hand out at the sea: the vast and lonely sea that surrounded our city, eating at its houses, cutting it off from the mainland. The sea was as black as the vast, empty seas of space my ancestors had once crossed. The Sons of Light thought that they could hide from the sea because they were afraid of it. Well, I was afraid of it too, but I realized then that it was something to be faced. I had thought the sea was mine when I was willing to turn my back on the mainland and all its luxuries, but I hadn't understood that the sea demanded another, bigger sacrifice.

"We'll manage," Pa said. "Somehow."

# 4
## THE GARDEN

IT WAS ONLY four weeks from the night that the Sons of Light told us they were deserting the Commune to the day when the fish would begin to run, but Pa said that I might just as well get as much schooling as I could. There was nothing to do but go. Erasmus McGuffey was the local schoolmaster who was responsible for teaching all the Silkies from the ages of six on up. But he acted more like the local missionary from the mainland trying to prepare us for the promised land: the mainland and its city life. If we had let him, he would have taken no pay at all without giving a thought to how he himself was going to eat. He taught his classes with a passion, as if he thought New Sion was paradise itself, but outside the schoolroom he always looked apologetic—like he was sorry that he didn't know the first thing about living in the old city.

Erasmus had his classes on the third floor of the old house where he lived. It wasn't a very big classroom, but then he never had very big classes, not more than ten kids at any one time even though there must have been some thirty signed up. Erasmus just acted like he did not mind and went on gamely, teaching from the books that he himself brought from the mainland—the old irreplaceable books with the spines getting just a little more cracked each year and the pages getting looser until Erasmus had to open the books as if they were flowers.

We sat around on the floor most of the time—or if the tide was up and the water was washing in, we stood. Aside from the shelves and an old slate blackboard there was not much furniture besides the odd assortment of chairs that had been donated to the school. The chairs were fragile and creaked an awful lot, so nobody got any work done while they were seated on them. So now Erasmus had all the chairs at the back of the room like they were guests lined up in even rows, watching Erasmus perform, as he called it.

Only that morning, we had not gotten more than started—and I had had my wrist slapped twice with the ruler for not paying attention—when we heard a steady, thunderous roar echoing down the old streets. We all jumped to the window, and it was all Erasmus could do to push his way to the window in time to see the giant silver sphere appear overhead. It must have been five hundred yards in diameter. Stars of light winked and danced on its smooth rounded sides and its shadow spread across the city like a stain, slipping down one wall, across the water, and up the wall on the other side. It floated on past the Commune and hung suspended over a spot to the northeast.

"That's Pa," Little Ham Dudum shouted. "And he brung Mr. Satin." Little Ham looked over at me and let out the big, loud laugh that I hated so much.

There were triumphant shouts from all the fool children that belonged to the Sons of Light, but the rest of us looked sober and the smarter ones of us looked scared. We watched until the buildings had shut out the sight of the ship. Erasmus looked tired when he turned from the window. He was a big, gaunt man. It had cost him a lot to come here and teach the Silkies, most of whom thought reading was a mainland madness. Now he spread his arms wide and herded us all from the window, shooing us like so many silly birds until we had all taken our places, and it took some hard rapping on his desk and on some knuckles before he had everyone in the class quieted down enough to continue the lesson. Only then Pa climbed up to the schoolroom and walked in, looking real solemn.

"That's all for today, Erasmus. All you kids go on home. Your folks'll tell you what to do."

Erasmus slammed his book shut impatiently, smoothing the precious pages back into the book. "Really, Captain Priest, I shouldn't have to dismiss my class for at least another four weeks."

"We need the children," Pa said. "Come on, Tyree."

And he turned his back on poor Erasmus, and I was up like a shot, because I was not about to have my wrist slapped any more that day. As soon as we were in our skiff you could hear the whole room explode with shouts and yells, and then there was the clomp and clatter of booted feet getting into boats, and poor Erasmus's voice trying to rise above the noise, trying to tell the children to leave in an orderly manner.

Pa did not say anything. I didn't dare ask him any questions after sneaking a look at him rowing in the bow, all solemn and grave. Caley and Ma had four cups of tea ready— the special tea that Ma treasured because it came from five light-years away. We drank it in silence, and only when everyone had finished did Pa speak.

"Tyree, Satin came faster than I thought. I've got to reorganize what's left of the Commune. Do you think you can take care of our garden from now on?"

It had been fun when Pa took me with him to work the garden. For the last three years I had been working the garden myself when Pa asked me to, but there was something about having to do it day in and day out that made me feel sad. When I had wanted to get out of school so I could work, I had had other kinds of work in mind, like salvaging or hunting. But Pa looked so tired and so worried that I wanted to take away some of his troubles.

"I will, sir," I said, and I think I managed to keep all the reluctance out of my voice.

Caley got up and stood before Pa. "And what about me?"

Pa took her on his lap, trying to make her smile. "You, young lady, can help your mother by taking care of the house."

"No," Caley said. "You said everyone had to help with the fish run. I can do something too."

Pa looked first at me and then at Ma, and I felt sorry for Pa, but I wasn't about to help him out. In some perverse way it made sense that if I had to grow up, so did Caley.

"You *are* doing something, dear." Ma tried to smooth Caley's hair. "By just staying home and being a good girl."

"No." Caley pushed Ma's hand away peevishly and she squirmed on Pa's lap. Her face grew uglier by the moment. "No." Until Pa suddenly lifted her off his lap and dropped her to her feet.

"You can't, Caley. You'd just be in the way!"

Caley didn't even cry—that was what made us feel so bad. If she had cried or screamed or thrown a tantrum, it would have been childish and understandable, but she crawled into her corner like a little hurt animal, or like a human being who is hurt deep down in her soul. She pulled her old blanket tighter about herself, just sitting hunched there, staring blindly toward the table; even when we all left it, she kept staring there just like we were still there.

Pa left then, not even bothering to eat anything—it was like he only wanted to escape from the house and Caley. Caley stayed in the corner in her sulk.

I didn't think I could eat at the table with her staring at me, so I thought I might just as well try to cheer her up. "What do you want me to bring back for you, Caley?"

"Nothing." She kicked out at me, but her foot got caught in the blanket and it slowed her down. But trying to avoid being kicked, I sat down hard, and that sound compensated her. She gave a little smug smile.

"Come on, sweetheart," Ma coaxed her. "We'll make dough men today."

Caley pulled her foot back under the blanket and pulled the blanket around her until it was as tight as a little cocoon.

"I can't see, remember?"

"All right, Misery, have it your way," Ma said impatiently. She stuffed some lunch into a little bag for me to take. For a moment, just for a moment, I felt like back-handing Caley because she ought to know better than to keep acting like she could see. I held my hand up ready to hit her, but Caley was oblivious to it, sitting quietly in her little patch of light, so instead of hitting her, my hand touched her cheek lightly.

"How about coming with me, Caley?" I asked. Ma was right beside me in a moment, and I could feel her own hand squeezing my shoulder lightly in gratitude.

"I'm not going along just for a ride?" Caley asked suspiciously.

" 'Course not. Everyone has to pull his weight now," I said. "You're going to be wishing you had stayed home today."

"All right," Caley said, scrambling to her feet.

Autumn was the most beautiful time of the year. Life simply exploded in the city: sea flowers and vines burst into bloom on the old stone so that the ruins melted into solid walls of color. The air was sweet with seeds floating sometimes like a mist above the water, and nectar dripped thick and amber down the vines, drawing bright scarlet insects out of the water to run shimmering up the old buildings.

Scarlet anemones spilled their young out into the streets so that the water turned red like wine—sea wine, Pa called it. At night, though, the phosphorescent water insects and tiny crabs came out so that the streets seemed to shimmer and glow as if the water were on fire. And if you went out at night, your paddle and the hull of the boat would become encrusted with shining jewel-like animals.

Sometimes I startled a lizard sunning itself on an old windowsill and it darted inside, dislodging a cloud of pebbles into the water, and other times some sea animal passed by us, his bubbles rising upward to break and send ripples that touched our bow.

First we went down to the winterberry patches, where the buildings had crumbled into the street. I tied up the boat and together we picked our way across the large, low mounds that were covered with green bushes. The steady buzz of insects filled our ears.

You were supposed to be careful not to burst the ripe berries when you plucked a bunch, but sometimes Caley cheated so she could suck the thick, creamy juice off her fingers. The juice was bittersweet—it made you frown a little and pucker—but the soothing feeling it gave your throat was worth it. As Ma said, sometimes to get something precious you had to take something else along with it.

When we finished filling our basket, I headed us out toward our garden. Caley liked to sit in the stern and watch the shadows dance in and out of the boat, because that much she can really see. Or maybe hang over the water enjoying that delicious empty dizziness, leaning over so far that I had to grab hold of her legs and tell her to sit down before she tipped us both into the water. Not that Caley could not swim—she could swim well enough—I just didn't have a mind to get too wet on a day like this.

Right then a flight of aircars passed overhead and I heard Little Ham's big booming laugh. The Sons of Light must have been moving out to their new homes that they'd been boasting about. They weren't much, just hemispheric shelters set up on the rooftops; but the Sons of Light counted them as palaces.

"What's the matter, Tyree?" Caley asked.

"Nothing, Cal."

"No," Caley said stubbornly. "I got a right to be told. I'm helping, you know."

Fuller Satin's ship had huge antigravity engines that kept it floating above the city. No matter where you were in the city, you could not escape it. It floated in the sky, looking as if it was ready to fall right on top of you; and when you turned your back on it, the feeling that it was going to crush you just got worse. The aircars began to swarm around it like flies. I wished mightily that I could knock it out of the sky.

"Tyree, you tell me this minute what you see," Caley insisted.

"Just Satin's ship and some aircars."

"Oh, them. I don't want to hear about them." Caley relaxed now. "Tell me a story, Tyree?"

"What kind of story, Caley?"

She frowned as if she had to make a choice, though every time she asked for the same thing—because there was only one story that Caley was really satisfied with. Sometimes I got kind of tired of telling the same story over and over, but today I kept patient.

"Tell me about what you see," she said.

"It's just buildings, Cal."

"No," she said. "Tell me what you really see."

"Well . . ." I looked around me for a long moment, picking up the scene. We were in a spot with a gentle current that would keep us in the middle of the street, so I could close my eyes and see like Caley. "I see the roofs of houses like golden rafts floating into the sky, and towers just like hands praying, and the water sparkles like blue glass."

"And the people," Caley said impatiently. "The people."

And for one moment, I could almost see them with Caley, as if one of our ancestors had seen this very same scene and his memory was coming back to us. It existed, this shining city of gold—if not here, then somewhere else in the universe. It was even more real than the old stone and brick surrounding us at that moment, because stone and brick are bound to fall apart, but the other city, the dream city, could live on long after this city was dust.

"They are tall people, musical people, beautiful people. They have little bells sewn to their capes and shoes, and they seem to dance when they move. Their voices ring musically and their gestures are all graceful. Heroes we'd call them nowadays."

I began to feel myself warming up. "And now the crowd parts and smiles light their faces and everyone is cheering. Down the street floats a golden barge. The sail is bright red. In the bow is a princess. In the stern, a prince . . ."

"And the music he's playing. Tell me about the music."

I opened my eyes to orient myself and saw Caley's hand dangling over the side. "Take your hand out of the water," I told her.

"Why?" she demanded.

"There are eels there that will think your fingers are just little worms, and they'll have your hand off with one bite." She turned her head to either side, listening, and then looked at me stubbornly.

"There aren't any eels here now."

"Well, there's other things," I said. "You know what Pa says about putting your hands into the water."

"And you know what Pa says about lying to me," Caley said.

"You are not supposed to take everything literally," I said, but Caley had gone into one of her sulks again. I tried coaxing her out of it but she would not listen, so I gave up.

And then Caley added, "And you may have two eyes, but you can hardly use your ears."

"What do you hear?" I demanded, but now it was Caley's

turn to smile maliciously and she sat back triumphantly in the stern.

"You see so well, you tell me."

"Come on, Cal." But she wouldn't say a word and I would not give her the satisfaction of begging, so the two of us went down the street, feeling about as guilty and frustrated as anyone can. And then even I could feel it, a sort of tingling along the fine hairs of my arms: something waiting for the two of us. Something horrible, though I told myself that Caley had only spooked me. But I hurried up toward our garden. And when we rounded the corner, we found a boat there ahead of us: a big twenty-footer, looking sleek and expensive and out of place in our old streets.

I could hear the laughing now, and Caley twisted this way and that, trying to find out what was happening, until finally her curiosity got the better of her and she looked at me. "What is it, Tyree?"

"A boat," I said. "A mainland boat."

I let the current pull the skiff in toward the garden and moored the skiff to the bolt ring. There were sounds of splashing and more shouts but I kept control of myself and made sure that I helped Caley out of the skiff. She did not let go of my hand but held it tightly, and she was trembling as we mounted the path to the top of the dam.

There were about ten Mainlanders there, dressed in what a mainland tailor thought were roughing outfits, though they were as gaudy and bright as parrots and with just about as much sense. There was only one man dressed for Old Sion and that was Big Ham Dudum in his wet suit, splashing around in our garden. Two of the Mainlanders were running around and every now and then squatting to take a picture of Dudum as he dove in and out of the garden, throwing bits of coral up onto the dam. The Mainlanders were encouraging him or picking up the coral and examining it with small exclamations.

Dudum climbed out of the water, sitting down on our dam. "Them's the Priest children. You wouldn't know it to look at them, but they're the children of the Captain here."

And one of the mainland women, the fat rolling and bulging through her outfit, started to coo obnoxiously. "Why, they're nothing but skin and bones."

"It doesn't help any," I said quietly, "when you ruin our food gardens."

"These gardens"—Big Ham held up his hand to the street—"belong to Mr. Satin. He's filed his claim all legal and everything."

"But they're ours. They have been ours for generations," Caley said.

One of the Mainlanders guiltily held out a dying flower-like worm still in its protective shell. "I thought these were just souvenirs."

The Mainlanders shifted around uncomfortably and then the man with the worm reached into his pocket and threw some coins. They fell on the rocks with tiny clinks, rolling and glistening. "Here, boy. We didn't know any better."

And the other Mainlanders threw coins, too, which arched through the air to fall with a hard metallic ring in front of us. A ten-credit piece clinked on the ground and circled right to my boot. An absolute fortune to any Silkie. I stared down at it.

"They're yours, boy," a woman said. And then one of the Mainlanders raised his camera to his eye to snap a picture of me and the money. If I had had enough spit in my mouth, I would have put it right into his lens. I was shaking, I was so mad, and then Caley pulled at my arm.

"Tyree," she whispered painfully. "Tyree. Please let's go."

I let her pull me down from the dam and with a great show of dignity we went back to the skiff. Behind us we could hear the tourists muttering.

"Why didn't he take the money?" one of them said, puzzled.

"Ain't got no sense," Big Ham said. "Just like claiming this garden was theirs."

I held the skiff steady for Caley and she climbed into it, holding on to my shoulders.

"Why, she's blind," the fat woman said from above.

"Let's go, oh, please, Tyree," Caley begged.

"Oh, Potiphar," the fat woman gushed, "get her picture." I could hear the camera already clicking away.

"How about if we follow the children for a bit," Dudum drawled. "Then you can see a typical day in the life of a Silkie."

I twisted around angrily in the bow of the skiff to see Dudum looking directly at me. He was smiling grimly as if to say, You ruined my day: I might as well ruin yours.

I've posed for pictures before, lots of times, because we have had our share of tourists in Old Sion, but they were polite enough to ask first, and then it was only one or two pictures and they had not come in trampling our garden. But these folks were following me around just as if they had a right to snoop on me and take little bits of my life on film.

I took us down the street as fast as I could, but the ship with its powerful engine was right on top of us a moment later, with the grinning Big Ham at the wheel. Every time I tried to row away from the boat, Big Ham would speed up so that his bow would be turning the water over just behind me. I noticed then that Big Ham had not wanted to bother his nice, sleek ship with protective nets the way all the Silkies did this time of year.

"Make them go away, Tyree," Caley said. She had her hands over her ears to try to shut out the whir of the Mainlander's camera. My arms were sore from rowing all day, but I sent the skiff on toward the purple water I had seen earlier.

"Smile at the camera," I said to Caley.

"What for?" she asked.

"Do as I say," I hissed. Caley and I waved hello at the Mainlanders. Then I sent the boat around a corner so fast that I heard Dudum rev up his big old engine to catch up to me and teach me a lesson. Only I grabbed hold of a projecting ledge as we turned the corner and held on tight so that the skiff banged against the wall.

The other boat shot around the corner, water spraying us and almost swamping us. "Tyree!" Caley shouted in fright.

"It's okay, Caley," I said. Too late Dudum saw he was heading into the purple water and killed his engine. But they drifted right into the middle of it.

The reason why we hang our boats with heavy nets during the autumn is because of purple patches just like that. The water turns purple because polyps are growing young ones. The moment they feel any large thing pass by, the younger polyps break away from their parents and shoot upward to attach themselves to the animal or the boat, hitching a free ride until they find some area they like. Then the polyps let go to start a new colony there. Our nets are impregnated with a juice made from crushed polyps, because the animals won't compete for an area if they can smell other polyps already there.

The tourists couldn't understand what Dudum was worried about. They had durillum armor, and they were in a boat guaranteed unsinkable with an engine powerful enough to outrun almost anything; and yet there was their guide cursing and swearing and trying to backwater. The sea churned all around the boat and the engine rose to an earsplitting roar, and the water started to boil with a purple spray as the propellors tossed up bits of little polyps. And then the engine stalled, choked by the polyps.

"Everything's all right, folks," Big Ham shouted as he made his way to the stern. "Everything's just fine." Laughing, I backed the skiff out of the street. Behind us I could hear Big Ham still telling the tourists not to worry.

After we finished laughing, we paddled along in companionable silence, letting the afternoon and the city slowly drift by as we headed for home.

"Tyree," Caley asked finally, "do you think they'll be all right?"

"A boat that big has got everything, including a radio. They can call for help any time—though," I added as an afterthought, "if they have to swim away from that ship they may have to pluck spare polyps off themselves for the rest of the week."

# 5

## THE NIGHT VIGIL

I TOLD PA everything when we got back, so the Commune was ready that evening when File Gribble, Big Ham, and Erech Tate came by. They didn't consider themselves under Pa's authority anymore, but Pa says it takes more than a tailor to change a man. Pa treated Big Ham's complaint the way he would have treated any Silkie's, and he kept them waiting until the Commune had gathered on the rooftops.

It was the last thing that File and Erech wanted, but they sat there like some Mainlander's idea of what starmen ought to look like: big six-foot dolls dressed up in cheap toy outfits. The uniforms were slick enough, all white plastic with gold buttons and braid. We didn't do anything but stare at the fools like they deserved—ten-cent wonders, Ma called them.

Pa stood on the podium of planks laid across concrete blocks. His own uniform was modeled after Great-Great-Grandpa's. Though his uniform was worn and patched here and there, Pa had a natural authority that no amount of money could buy. Pa looked around at the faces, faces he had known since he was a boy, faces with features that had been common among us for over three centuries: stern faces lined with too much hard work and too little reward.

"All right," Pa said finally. "You all know what happened this afternoon."

Big Ham got up then like a man who had been working up his nerve all that afternoon and had not done too well. "Those gardens had to be protected by legal title."

"I didn't hear about your Great-Great-Grandpa helping my Great-Great-Grandpa build my garden," Shadrach Lawson said.

"No, nor helping mine," Benteen Heth shouted from where he was sitting. There was an angry stir in the Commune just like a wind blowing across ivy on the face of a building.

Erech Tate jumped up. "Dang it! Be honest with me, Shadrach. Don't you spend at least ten hours away from home, every day, without a holiday?"

"I ain't never complained," Shadrach said.

"Well, maybe it's about time you did," Tate snapped. "You gotta go out hunting and salvaging. Your kids most likely got to do the same and work the garden with your missus. Your family probably don't get together for more than an hour or two every night before you have to go to sleep. Now tell the truth."

"It's a good way," Shadrach said defensively.

"But we got a better way." Big Ham held up a thick sheaf of paper credits and waved them in the air so that they rattled. "I got compensation here for all of you."

"That's going to make a mighty poor meal if that's all you've got to eat this winter," said Jafer Purdy beside me. There were loud laughs at that and some voices urging Jafer on.

"No, you dang fool." Big Ham shook his head. "You buy

food with this, more food than you'll be able to eat."

"And where do you buy this food? Twenty miles over in New Sion?"

"No," Big Ham announced triumphantly. "Mr. Satin, he's opening up a commissary right here."

"That's what I figured," Pa said quietly. "That's fine for this year, Ham, but what about next year? And the year after that? Is Mr. Satin going to compensate me every year?"

Big Ham dropped his hand back by his side and he sagged just a little, but Tate started to bristle like a porcupine fish. "Have some pity for your family, Priest."

"I'm still the Captain, Tate," Pa said quietly. His words brought Tate up short. "You call me 'sir.'"

File made Tate and Dudum both sit down. "Captain, you need something for this winter. You might just as well take this money. Please, you deserve it."

"If my boy wouldn't take your mainland money, what makes you think I would?" Pa asked.

"But what about your garden?" Javan Fitch protested.

Pa shrugged. "As far as I can see, we have been out-flanked by the law." There were angry, hurt shouts from some but Pa waved down the noise and went on talking. "Now, shouting won't get back your land, so I asked Erasmus today to visit New Sion and file some new claims. He'll ask some of his university friends to see that everything is done legal."

"You want us to start over?" asked Mash Purdy, Jafer's father, in dismay.

Pa shrugged. "A little exercise wouldn't harm any of us, but that ain't the point of the assembly. There's a Silkie by the name of Tyree Priest who damaged another Silkie's boat."

"Forget it, Captain," File said. File motioned to Big Ham to be quiet. "We ain't Silkies anymore, remember?"

"File, you may look in the mirror and see someone different, but I see the same File Gribble that I grew up with," Pa said in a quiet voice. "Now, as I see it, the only thing Tyree Priest is guilty of is not warning Dudum about the purple patch in time."

"I said forget it, Captain," File insisted. "We ain't Silkies no more."

Big Ham, though, had stood all he could. I suppose he was more mad at the other Silkies than at me but I was the closest thing at hand. "Shut up, File. Whether I'm a Silkie or an outsider, the boy still done me wrong."

"He didn't do anything I wouldn't have done," Benteen shouted.

And then old Tubal Kahn stood up. "You're lucky that's all Tyree did to you," Tubal said and sat down again, because for him that was a long speech. He looked content and so did most everyone else except for the Sons of Light.

"You're the Captain," Big Ham went on. "What are you going to do about it?"

"You mean, when one Silkie hurts another? Why, I'll punish Tyree, of course." Pa stilled the angry muttering. "We'll make Tyree stand the first watch tonight."

I could have jumped up and shouted for joy. I was only thirteen and I had expected it to take another five years before I could stand watch. There are a lot of noises in the night that you have to learn to ignore, and also a lot of soft noises that you have to alert the whole Commune about. It meant, too, that I would get a watch knife. I was sitting with my friends, and they pounded me on the back and whooped till it was a wonder I had any back or ears left.

About the only other person besides Big Ham that didn't look pleased was Ma. She just sat on the bench picking nervously at her fingers.

When I look back at it now, Pa was pretty clever about my watch. He had to do some reshuffling in order to let me stand watch that night, and he saw to it that only the best and truest men stood watch with me—Tubal Kahn and Benteen Heth and Shadrach Lawson.

The three of them stood in our front room an hour later, watching solemnly while Ma packed me a snack. She had taken out Pa's best, warmest cloak for me to wear and was bustling around with a hundred other things she wanted done before she'd let me go. Caley sat excitedly on the edge of a chair while I stood, trying to lean casually against the wall like I had done this a hundred times before. I already had my hunting spear, but Pa was upstairs getting my knife.

"Now, Tyree, don't you go running to investigate every sound, you hear? I mean, it's dark up on those roofs, even with the torches," Ma was saying. I nodded every few seconds but I was too excited to listen and slightly embarrassed that the rest of the watch had to hear everything. Though if any of them thought it was funny, not one of them let on.

Then Pa was downstairs, smiling in his own quiet way, with the knife wrapped up in some old brown cloth. "Sorry I kept you waiting, gentlemen. I wanted to sharpen the knife up some."

Ma looked up in alarm like she was afraid I was going to cut myself a lot easier now, but all us men pretended like we didn't notice her fright. Instead we all watched Pa as he carefully dropped the folds of cloth to reveal the knife.

"But that's Great-Great-Grandpa's," I said.

"And the truest-balanced, sharpest-edged knife you ever saw, Tyree," Pa said. He smiled when I lifted it reverently, admiring how the light ran down the edges of the blade. The knife was really long enough to be called a short sword. It had a beautiful blade of New Bethlehem steel with pieces of horn inlaid on the hilt. The knife was so well balanced that it seemed as if made from light and air: it was that easy to hold.

There were deadly curses etched on the blade, in another old Terran language besides Anglic, to finish off someone if the blade did not do the job. Erasmus had once started to translate them but had stopped because he said he was afraid his tongue would blister. Then Pa asked him to write the words down, only Erasmus said the paper would probably burn up too, which seemed to me as interesting a thing to see as to actually learn the curses. But Erasmus still refused.

"It's a good weapon," Tubal announced solemnly, and the others nodded. I looked at Pa with a silent question. He read my mind and nodded.

"It's yours now, Tyree."

I sheathed it happily, feeling suddenly a stranger to everyone, feeling as if our home, this city, was too small for me. When Ma finally ran out of things to do and it was time for us to go, Pa just gripped my shoulder lightly.

"I've a feeling that Big Ham hasn't forgotten, so be careful tonight. All of you."

And with that he sent the four of us to our posts, one at

each corner of the Commune area.

It was a solemn night. I don't think there will ever be another night when I will feel so important as I did pacing my rounds on the rooftop, with the stars cold and hard above me and the sea shining in the street below so that a ghostly light played up the walls to the very edge of the rooftop. And behind me the whole Commune was dark and quiet except for the one light in our house where I knew Ma was staying up. But even that could not rob me of the pleasure of walking my rounds, alone with all the safety of the Commune upon my shoulders.

That was when I heard a low sigh behind me. I whirled about, crouched, with my spear pointed toward the sound.

"Lord, boy, be careful with that fish-sticker, will you?"

I straightened up, relieved and angry at the same time. "Amadeus?"

The old Argan shuffled out of the shadows into the torch-light where his faceted eyes made a hundred torches gleam and wink on his face. "I almost didn't recognize you," he said. Under one arm-leg he had his trumpet. "You look fine that way, Tyree. Real fine."

"I won't take back the trumpet, Amadeus," I warned him.

"Didn't come here for that," Amadeus said proudly. "I came to pay you back—with the Seadragon's treasure."

I could feel my insides growing brittle. "Amadeus, this wouldn't have anything to do with teasing the Seadragon, would it?"

"We weren't teasing her, Manchild. We were a-lurin' her away from the cove where she sleeps, so Sebastian could fetch her treasure."

"But I thought Argans hated water."

"We do, but that doesn't mean we can't dive deep when there's a need; and only the Seadragon's most precious treasure could pay you back for this." Amadeus patted the trumpet affectionately.

I stared for a long time at Amadeus. I didn't like to think that I was indirectly responsible for making the Sons of Light leave, but there wasn't anything else to do but face it. But Amadeus was so busy talking that he did not notice how bothered I was.

"Lord, Manchild, but it's worth a whole song in itself—with us distracting the Seadragon and Sebastian doing his deep dives. He had to go down three times. But it's worth it. Why, there isn't the like of this treasure within a hundred light-years. People'll come from all around just to admire—"

"Stop it, Amadeus."

Amadeus cocked his head to one side. "What's wrong, Manchild?"

"I can't accept the Seadragon's treasure."

Amadeus clicked to himself in Argan for a moment. "Why not?"

I explained to him about how the Seadragon had scared the Sons of Light into selling out and how they were bringing in Satin.

Amadeus puffed up his cheeks in annoyance and then blew them out with a loud sigh. "That's too bad, Manchild. But I'll tell you: Giving the Seadragon's treasure back to her won't bring those fool Manchildren back into your Commune again, so why don't you take the treasure?"

"Well, I just can't."

"Have a look at it first," Amadeus suggested hopefully.

"No, Amadeus." I set my jaw in the stubborn way of the Priests.

Amadeus cradled the trumpet in four of his hand-feet like it was his own child, but finally he held it out to me. "Will you take back the trumpet then?"

"Knowing what it means to you?" I shook my head. "You know I couldn't."

"Well, Lord God of hosts, if I ever heard the like of Manchildren sense." Full of self-righteous indignation, he spread out two arm-legs. "We risk life and limb—not to mention getting wet—in order to get the treasure. We do all this and then you won't take it."

"I'm sorry, Amadeus, but I really can't take the treasure, so please don't be mad at me."

He glanced at me and then looked down at the trumpet uncomfortably. He went on grumbling to himself for another minute or two, mostly in Intergal so I could understand how irritated he was, but eventually he gave a massive shrug of six of his shoulders. "We'll talk about this some other time. Meanwhile, why don't you see what else we found?"

"What is it?"

"It's two things. Come and see them," Amadeus said. I followed him reluctantly to the next rooftop.

There lay Big and Little Ham, trussed up and gagged with tough, unbreakable Argan fibers. They squirmed frantically when they saw me but I paid them no mind. I went over to where the Argans had piled the Dudums' equipment; it wasn't for night fishing. They had ropes and some reeds split fine at one end to form switches, and I could just guess who they had been going to try them on.

"You were going to beat me, weren't you?" I asked Big Ham. He shook his head frantically from side to side, but his frightened eyes gave the lie to that.

"By rights," I said, "I could put this spear right between your shoulder blades and not have to take any blame." It was a cheap enough victory to see them squirm, trying to break free, and I knew immediately how cheap it was. "But I won't," I added.

For a moment I was inclined to leave them up on the rooftop until somebody found them, but that seemed too cruel. "Amadeus," I said. "Will you take these gentlemen home?"

"I suppose," Amadeus drawled.

"And maybe you better retie them with their own ropes so there won't be any clues as to who did it."

Amadeus consulted with his nephews and all the Argans made clicking sounds and snapped their finger-toes, punc-tuated by a furious stamping of hand-feet. I should have been suspicious when they used Argan talk—as for the Sons of Light, they looked genuinely frightened of the aliens. Amadeus turned around with a twinkle in his eyes. "You know this makes the second gift you tried to turn down," he warned. "But we'll help you with this at least."

I hurried back to my station, feeling pretty miserable. Like I said before, ever since I could remember I had waited for this one night when I would stand my own watch, because that would be a sure sign that I had grown up. Only now that my first watch night had finally come, I found that I didn't want to grow up. As long as I was just a boy, I could tell Pa when I did something wrong and he would give me my punishment and then everything would be all right again. But now I didn't see how I could ever fix things like they used to be. It gave me a shivery kind of feeling and I felt old, terribly old.

# 6

## THE TOUCHSTONE

I WAS RELIEVED at about midnight with "nothing" to report to Pa. I had a hard time deciding not to say anything, but I really wanted to think about things. I didn't sleep very well that night. And I spent most of the next day rehearsing the routine of the fish run, but I kept on brooding about the night before and I can't say that I remembered much.

On the one hand, I was sorry for what I had done to the Silkies, and yet on the other hand I was glad I had learned Argan music. No matter how much I tried, I just could not resolve the two. I was so busy with my own problems that the news at dinnertime came as a shock. Pa told us that some Argans had attacked a group of tourists that afternoon.

"Wasn't there a Silkie with the tourists?" Ma asked.

"That's the dangedest thing about it," Pa said. "The Dudums breezed right into Sheol—like they were just itching to use their guns."

I sat up anxiously in my chair. "Was anybody hurt?"

"No," Pa said. "The Argans are too clever for that." Pa chuckled. "But there is one party of tourists that is badly scared and a mighty big ammunition bill for Fuller Satin. I hear they fired off nearly a thousand rounds and shot up walls, fish, and shadows all the way back to his ship."

"What's gotten into those Dudums, I wonder," Ma said. "You wouldn't think they'd lose *all* their common sense."

"Well," Pa said, "I did hear one story about Big and Little Ham being found tied up in some lady's tent but I don't believe it. I mean, Purdy told me they were stark naked."

"Naked?" Caley giggled loudly.

"Except for the ropes they were wearing," Pa said.

Mentally I bawled out the Argans for going too far. No wonder the Dudums had gone into Sheol. They were just primed to get even.

Ma was shaking her head. "You're right. I don't believe it."

Pa wiped at his mouth with his handkerchief and smiled. "And what's more, they claim it was Argans that done it to them."

"That clinches it for sure," Ma said. "Those boys ought to know better than to stretch their story that far."

"It's so outrageous there may be some truth in it." Pa shrugged.

"Naked." Caley giggled until Ma told her to hush up.

Pa left too fast after supper for me to do much thinking on whether to tell him everything or not—about the Argans and my flute lessons and everything. There was no telling how he might take it. But things were getting worse while I kept my secret.

I had to do some more thinking, so I told Caley to go to bed. I walked around and then sat by the balcony, trying to decide one way or the other. I wasn't ready for the touch of a warm soft hand and I jumped.

"It's awfully cold up here, Tyree," Caley said. "How come you don't have a fire going?"

"I forgot," I said and sat down. "How come you're not in bed?"

"Couldn't sleep with you stomping around overhead. You'd think you wanted to kick the house down."

"Well, I won't pace anymore, so go to bed." I gave her a little squeeze and tried to push her but she stood there stubbornly.

"What's the matter, Tyree? Can't you tell me?"

"I can't figure out a sentence in the logbooks," I lied.

Caley's fingers tightened around my arm. "Don't you lie to me, Tyree Priest. The cap's still on your lamp. You haven't been at your desk the whole time."

"Will you mind me and go to bed?" I gave her an exasperated shove and she stumbled against the desk. She must have bruised something because she let out a little hiss. I got out of my chair right away. "Cal, are you okay?"

Caley retreated into her listening corner. "Don't you touch me, Tyree. I guess I got as much right to be up here as you do."

I closed the balcony doors and gathered logs for a small fire in the fireplace. "It's awfully cold up here, Cal."

"Umph. I knew that when I came up here, which is a lot more than you can say for some folk."

I poked the logs till I had them placed just right and then lit the kindling with flint and steel. "Wouldn't you like to sit by me?"

"Umph."

I sat down before the fireplace and pretended to let out

a weary sigh. "You don't have to, but I'd appreciate it if we could snuggle up together for a bit till the fire warms the room."

"Umph."

"Please, Cal."

"You're spoiled rotten, you know that?" Caley got up though and sat down beside me, pulling in her skinny legs and settling herself against me.

I put my arm around her. "It's not that I don't want to tell you, Caley. It's just that I can't."

"At least tell me who's visiting you?"

"Visiting?"

"There's someone up here. I heard him coming down the stairs from the rooftop. That's why I came up." Caley turned her sensitive ears toward her left. "He's right outside now."

I could hear the soft shuffling of hand-feet on the landing.

"Amadeus?" I called.

"Right here, Manchild." Amadeus stepped into the middle of the room. He tapped one hand-foot on the floor uncomfortably. In two of his middle hand-feet I saw what looked like a blue marble cube.

"He's not human," Caley said excitedly. Before I could speak, she had jumped up and was groping for Amadeus. "Is it an Argan? Is it?"

"Caley, mind your manners," I said. She was so used to being able to touch other people's faces that she didn't think anything of touching Amadeus. Instead of being angry or shy, though, Amadeus almost smiled—or came as close to smiling as I had ever seen.

"It's all right, Manchild," he said. Caley had put him at his ease. He waited patiently while Caley's fingertips brushed his head fur.

"Caley, he's not a cat," I said. She treated this old song-smith and Ultimate Uncle like he was just a house pet, but he took it calmly and even seemed to like it.

"I'll tell you when it bothers me." Amadeus settled his bulk down on the rug and stretched out his long knobby legs. He gave a sigh as Caley stroked his fur. "A little more to the right."

"He feels so soft," Caley said, and she knelt down beside Amadeus and slipped her arms around his neck and gave him a quick squeeze.

"Caley," I said.

"There's no way a little child could harm an Argan, except maybe rub off some hair. Hey now, you wouldn't hurt old Amadeus, would you?"

" 'Course not," Caley said indignantly.

"Amadeus, I ain't got time to fool around," I said. "I won't take the trumpet or the Seadragon's treasure."

"Treasure?" Caley asked even more excitedly. Caley's hands found the marble cube—at least I thought it was marble because it was white with blue veins streaking through it; but when she took it from Amadeus, I saw the cube was too light to be any rock because she could balance it on her fingertips.

"Oh," Caley said breathlessly. Her mouth formed silent little O's but nothing came out. Her look of amazement changed to a puzzled frown. The next instant, when she turned the cube over in her hands, her face shone with pure delight. A little shiver went up her back and she hugged the cube against her chest. She could not seem to stop stroking the different faces of the cube, and all the time the strangest expressions passed over her face.

"What is it, Caley?" I asked.

She spoke to me dreamily. "It's . . . oh . . . it's a touchstone."

I grabbed the cube angrily from Caley's hands. "We don't want—" I stopped in midsentence because I felt the weirdest sensations. My left hand touched what felt like silk while my right touched something like velvet. Then my left hand felt little fibers brushing and rubbing against its palm. My right hand felt as if something like water was trickling through my fingers, but when I held up that hand it wasn't wet.

"Give it back to me, Tyree. Give it back." Caley knelt and leaned forward with her arms outstretched. I held the touchstone over my head and her fingers desperately searched through the empty air. She almost seemed in a panic and her face began screwing up as if she were ready to cry. "Please, Tyree, please."

There was no denying the urgency in her voice. What could I say or do that would make up to her for the loss of the touchstone? Caley's hands grabbed my tunic. She couldn't even put her pleas into words anymore. She just made little sounds from her throat like a small, hurt animal. While I held the cube behind me in my left hand, I tried to hold her off with the right, but she would not stop. She threw herself forward, grabbing and pulling at my left arm. I pushed her away and held her against the floor.

"Damn it. Stop that, Cal!"

She lay quiet on the floor where I had put her. She just seemed to collapse and began to cry. I could see that touching things meant as much to Caley as music meant to me. To

Caley the touchstone was more than a toy; it was an entire world of sensations which she could hold in her hands. To Caley the touchstone was the equivalent of a great novel or a beautiful painting or a lovely and delicate symphony.

Life had not been fair to Caley. Erasmus once said that the Mainlanders had a special school just to teach the blind how to live a normal life; but we never had the money to send Caley and none of us had the know-how to teach her ourselves.

"Here," I said roughly and gave the touchstone to her. Caley sat up while she cradled the touchstone against her chest and rubbed her cheek against one face of the cube.

"I'll be good from now on, Tyree, I promise."

"Never you mind," I said. Right now Caley meant what she said, but I didn't put much trust in what she'd do tomorrow. I turned to Amadeus instead.

It was strange. I had hardly talked with Amadeus about my family, and yet he knew that Caley would be my one weak spot and had taken advantage of that fact. But then I guess you don't get to be an Ultimate Uncle without some kind of ability to understand people. Even so, I couldn't help resenting the way he had got around me.

"What's wrong, Manchild?" Amadeus asked gently.

"Amadeus, I told you that I didn't want to be paid back for the trumpet. Why did you trick me?"

Amadeus spoke in a very hurt tone. "It was something the Ultimate Uncle had to do, Tyree. That should be enough."

"That might satisfy some Argan but not a human. I want to know why you insisted on going to all that trouble."

"You know I don't talk about my reasons," Amadeus

snapped. "I like my privacy."

"You didn't respect my wishes about not being paid. I don't see why I have to respect yours about your almighty privacy. Just how old are you?"

"Old enough." Amadeus wouldn't look at me but watched the dying fire instead.

"Caley and I read about this Argan who once learned how to play the trumpet—"

"He was a shameful case," Amadeus said hurriedly. "A real shameful one. We don't like to talk about him much."

"Was he some kinsman of yours?"

Amadeus did not answer but drew his arm-legs protectively about himself.

"Was he?" I asked again.

"We were close." Amadeus spoke as if each word had been pulled out of his mouth with a pair of pliers.

"And he was the one who taught you how to play the flute and trumpet?"

"He was full of Manchildren notions like that. He couldn't stop asking questions—just like some other folk I know."

"But where did he get a trumpet and a flute from? I mean, when he taught you how to play them?"

"I told you that it ought to be enough that I could teach you."

"I just wanted to know, Amadeus," I said. "I don't think there's anything to be ashamed of. My stars, I'm the one that ought to be ashamed. It was my race that made fun of him."

"We don't want your pity," Amadeus said stiffly. He put his hand-feet on his knees and stood up as quickly as his age and sense of dignity would let him.

"Come on now, Amadeus," I said. "Don't be so touchy."

"Who's touchy?" Amadeus demanded.

"You are, you fool Argan."

"So I'm a fool now," Amadeus grunted.

"Well, I never. If ever there was a touchy person, you're the one."

"You'd be touchy too if some fool Manchild kept pestering you all the time."

"All right, then, I won't pester you. I've got better things to do than to play the flute with a bunch of old spiders."

Amadeus made an angry hissing sound when he heard the word "spiders." He tried to suck in his belly a little and he made his hand-feet into fists.

"Amadeus, I'm sorry. I didn't mean it. Honest." I looked at him pleadingly, and though Amadeus unballed his fists, he still stood rigidly.

"No use apologizing for that," Amadeus said. "You might just as well say you're sorry you gave me the trumpet or sorry about what the Mainlanders did to that shameful Argan or sorry your kind ever came to this world."

"That covers just about everything," I said, "but I'll apologize for all that if you want me to."

Amadeus widened his faceted eyes so I could see the hundreds of tiny Tyrees reflected there. I felt myself being weighed on some vast, imponderable scale to which this one angry moment was only a minute addition. "There's no reason to apologize for what you are," he said.

"I'll take back my words then," I said hurriedly.

"You know you can never do that," he said and lowered his eyelids slightly. He turned and vanished into the shadows of the balcony. I knelt there by the fireplace for a long time, wanting to call Amadeus back to me or to go after him myself, and yet I wasn't sure it would do any good.

Caley touched my arm timidly. "Tyree, you can have the touchstone back if you want."

"No, Cal," I said. "You keep it now."

"Tyree, did you really go into Sheol?" Cal asked breathlessly.

"Yes."

"And did you really learn how to play the flute?"

"Kind of."

"Will you play for me sometime?"

"I don't know if I can," I said. "I can play in front of the Argans but I think I'd feel funny playing in front of my own kind."

"Even in front of me?"

"Especially you. I would want to be really great for you and if I couldn't do that, well, I wouldn't want to do it at all."

"I understand. I won't ask again. You just tell me when you feel like playing." She kissed me lightly and I never loved Caley more than at that one moment.

I heard the *clink, clonk, clink* of Ma's clogs. She buys them special from the mainland where they still have trees for such purposes. "Caley, don't you tell them where the whatever-it-is—"

"Touchstone," Caley insisted.

"Don't you tell them where we got the thing from."

"It's a touchstone," Caley said as if that settled that. She put it reluctantly underneath my desk.

Ma pulled her robe tighter about her neck when she

came into the room. "What are you two doing up here at this time of the night and with only that tiny fire?"

"Tyree was just telling me about the stars, Mama," Caley said quickly. It was a feeble enough story, but Caley knew how to put just the right touch of innocence in her voice when she wanted to. Even I was almost taken in by the way she talked.

"Well," Ma said, mollified, "that can wait for warmer nights." She came over to pick up Caley but stopped short when she saw the touchstone under my desk. "What on earth is that?" She turned on me. "And don't you go telling me it dropped out of the stars, you Tyree."

It was awkward downstairs. Pa didn't say much but from the way he looked at me and Caley, you could tell he was hurt. He had gotten into the habit of being the Captain of the Commune, the direct heir of an unbroken chain of command that extended through three centuries. His pride had already been hurt by the Sons of Light, without his son keeping secrets from him.

"Mind telling me where you got that thing from?"

"It was a trade, Pa. I traded the trumpet to a friend for it."

"And who was that friend?"

"Just a friend," I shrugged.

"But who? Who could possibly want a trumpet?"

I kept quiet even when Ma sat down beside Pa. "Answer your father, Tyree."

I wanted to tell them everything real bad, but I was scared now. "Ma'am, I can't."

"Tyree, don't you be disrespectful to your father," Ma warned, but Pa waved his hand.

"If Tyree don't trust me, I won't force him."

"Pa, it ain't that way," I protested. "I mean, I just can't tell."

But Pa ignored me like I was already dead to him. He looked at Caley instead. She sat in her favorite corner with a mixture of awe and bliss on her face while she ran her fingers over the touchstone.

"What do we do about that thing, Inigo?" Ma glanced over at the touchstone. Her expression was a mixture of distaste, wonder, and fear. "I think it's alive."

"It is alive," Caley insisted.

Pa scratched the back of his head. "Well, maybe it is and maybe it isn't. Do you know how to feed it, Jerusha?"

"No," Ma was finally forced to admit.

"Well, until it starts demanding something to eat, I don't see why Caley can't keep it," Pa said. He pushed himself from the chair like he had aged twenty years in the last half hour, and Ma, she looked at me accusingly like I had added those years onto him.

# 7

## SATIN'S TEMPTATION

THE NEXT DAY, with Ma and Pa being so put out, I spent most of my time at home keeping quiet and helping with all the odd little things that had to be done for the fish run. There were nets to be repaired and food to be prepared, like cakes of ground fish meal and other quick meals.

The work had always been exciting to Caley before this, but now she resented the time spent away from her touchstone. If you made the slightest unexpected noise in the house, she would turn around and demand to know what it was—and if you did not tell her right away, she went into one of her magnificent sulks.

That was why none of us paid much attention to her when she straightened in her chair. "What was that?"

"Nothing, Caley." Ma went on packaging the dried seaweed that we would snack on. "Or were you kicking your sister under the table again, Tyree?"

"No," Caley said. "It wasn't Tyree. It was a sobbing sound like a giant crying far, far away."

"It's just the wind," Ma said.

Then Pa clambered over the balcony railing, pulling his

jerkin over his head. "Get my cap and coat, Jerusha. Some air-cars are coming toward here. I think it's Satin."

"But why would he come?" Ma asked, startled.

"There are still some Silkies left," Pa said.

"Yes. Of course," Ma said hurriedly. "Caley, you fetch Pa's cap and shine it up some while I get the coat."

Caley jumped off her chair in a second and went right to the pegs on the wall to lift down the old cap. She had to stand on tiptoe and search around a little on the wall, but she found it. Then with the hem of her dress she set to polishing the visor.

Then we could all hear the roar, a sobbing, rhythmic sound of air sucked between the giant rotors of aircars.

"See?" Caley went on polishing the visor. "What did I tell you?"

Ma came down with the coat, brushing it worriedly and frowning. "I didn't have time to get this spot out, Inigo."

"That's all right." Pa smiled. "Why, this visor's so shiny that I'll just keep it turned toward old Satin. That'll blind him for sure."

And he took the cap and coat, with thanks to the ladies, just as the shadows of the aircars went sliding up the street. The air-cars dropped almost directly out of the sun. They were oval in shape, about twenty-five feet long and eight feet wide. There was a rotor at each end and between the rotors was the box-shaped passenger compartment which was open to the air. Each had two seats which could hold seven people comfortably besides the pilot. The huge rotors chopped the water, sending sheets of spray rippling up and down the street and rattling against the windows. The light was slick on their sides as they settled onto the water, rocking gently back and forth in the swells they had made.

"Drop the ladder, Tyree," Pa said from behind me. I went to the balcony and pushed the ladder over the railing. The first aircar eased in toward our building with a blast of water jets until the end of the ladder rapped the side of the passenger compartment.

Dudum was the first one out, looking awfully satisfied with himself, even though he was having a hard time keeping his balance on the aircar while he held the ladder. He was about the only one who did not realize how foolish he looked.

Then Fuller Satin got out. You would have thought that he would have the decency to look degenerate or brutal, but he actually looked kind of pleasant—if overnice. He was a small, slender man, simply if expensively dressed. He nodded his thanks to Ham and climbed up the ladder cautiously. Really, Satin looked more like a school-teacher than Erasmus did. I couldn't say the same for Satin's friends, though. There was a tall, dark, scowling man who stood in the corner of the room, looking us all over with quick eyes.

It was a shock to see Erasmus come up the ladder. He was dressed in an old suit and an old hat—which were still better than anything we had ever been able to give him. The big man stepped to one side of the doorway, apologizing silently for his clothes and trying his best to look his usual shabby self—and not succeeding.

Satin shook hands with Pa like it was a great pleasure. "How do you do, sir," he said enthusiastically. "I can't tell you how delighted I am to be in your city."

"It's more your city now than ours," Pa said coldly.

Fuller held on to Pa's hand and patted it with his other hand. "An unfortunate misunderstanding, I can assure you, Captain."

Dudum came up over the railing then, grinning from ear to ear like a boy who has brought along his big brother to beat you up. "These is the Priests, Mr. Satin."

"Yes, yes." Mr. Satin nodded eagerly. "We've already introduced ourselves."

Ma looked at Pa, who shrugged. "Won't you come in, Mr. Satin?" she asked.

"Delighted," Mr. Satin said. "And, please, you must call me Fuller." He took Ma by the arm and looked around at the rest of us. "And this must be Tyree and this"—he turned to Caley—"must be your daughter. The likeness is obvious. . . ."

And I won't go on with the rest of what he said all through lunch, though I will say that Ma turned out a fine big meal for such short notice. But I knew what a dent it made in our larder, and I could see Pa figuring out how much side fishing we'd have to do to fill it up again. Anyway, Fuller Satin just went on and on with that obnoxious, meaningless talk, until I kept hoping he would put another mouthful of food into his mouth so he couldn't talk. It was nearly half an hour after the meal before Fuller Satin finally got around to the purpose of his visit.

"I understand, Captain Priest, from Mr. McGuffey"— Satin nodded toward Erasmus—"that you sent him to New Sion to file claim on some land."

"I didn't send him," Pa said. "He volunteered."

"Of course he did, like the worthy man he is." Satin

106

looked reflectively at his nails. "But that was not really necessary, you know."

"We wouldn't want to trespass on 'your' land, Mr. Satin," Pa said.

"Fuller, please," Mr. Satin said for the tenth time. "Let us say that Dudum became carried away in his zeal to show a good time to my friends. It won't happen again and I can assure you that you'll be fully compensated."

"That won't be necessary," Pa said formally. "We had no idea that the street would belong to you when our ancestors started the gardens."

"Yes, well—" Fuller Satin looked genuinely pained. "I did it to protect you, you know, against unscrupulous land developers."

Ma sniffed at that. The rest of us kept silent, because no comment was really necessary.

Fuller Satin shifted uncomfortably in his chair. "There are folk, don't you see, who wouldn't appreciate the beauties of your city and who would tear things down wholesale to construct another New Sion here."

"What about Tubal Kahn?"

"I have already seen Mr. Kahn and explained to him that it was all an unfortunate misunderstanding. Why, I've even proposed that he supply my restaurants with his produce." Satin leaned forward eagerly now. "You see, I will keep all my guests in my ship floating on antigravity above the city. No guest will sleep in the city from now on. This way both you and they may live as you're used to."

"I won't make myself or mine be clowns for anyone, Mr. Satin," Pa said quietly.

"Clowns, my friends?" Satin said, startled. "Why, I'd never treat my friends like clowns. These gifts are just a few tokens of my esteem." Fuller Satin folded his hands on his lap while File and the other Sons of Light put the presents on the table. None of us took kindly to the spectacle of Silkies acting like servants for us.

But the gifts were grand ones. There was a magnificent gun for Pa, a double-action, hand-tooled, hand-worked shotgun with a stock inlaid with ivory, looking more like a statue than a gun. For Ma there were flame silks from Nifl that changed color at the slightest change in temperature so that when you wore them, they changed color as you moved. And for me—well, I guess the Sons of Light had told Satin about me—for me there was a flute, a beautiful, gleaming silver flute with stops, that came in its own case. All you had to do was put the three pieces together.

Caley ran her hands through the flame silks. "Oh, Mama, Mama, feel them," she cooed. It hurt Pa to disengage Caley's hands.

"Thank you, Mr. Satin, but no, thank you."

"But Papa," Caley protested. "These are gifts."

"Precisely," Fuller Satin said.

"You can only take gifts from friends," Pa explained to both of them.

"You still won't believe that I'm your friend, will you, Captain Priest?" Satin shook his head sadly. "I've as much at stake in preserving Old Sion as you have."

"One or two visitors is fine, but twenty people at a time— if even twenty people come every month, Old Sion can never be as it was."

"I'll keep them far enough away, Captain Priest."

"No."

"I understand, Captain Priest. You're a proud man—just like my father." Satin smiled slyly. And all of a sudden I realized that he was a spoiled boy—and a dangerous one because he had all that money. "Well, maybe if you won't believe that I'm a friend, at least you should believe I mean well." He turned to the sour-looking man. "I brought along a friend that might, just might, be able to help Caley see."

"We have no money to pay a doctor," Pa said stiffly.

Satin waved his hand in dismissal. "The doctor's just an old school friend who happened to be visiting me, so he doesn't mind at all, do you, Doctor?"

"No," the doctor said. He turned to the Sons of Light and took his black bag from one of them. He came forward, looking apologetic. "If I could have a dark room."

"Upstairs," Ma said. She put her arm protectively around Caley as they walked up the stairs.

Satin said a lot of things that I don't remember because Pa and I were too busy listening to the feet moving above us, and then the doctor came back down. He had lost that sullen look he'd had when he left with Caley, because she must have taken his mind off Satin. But the moment he came back down and saw Satin again, the doctor lost his smile.

"Well?" Satin asked eagerly.

"It will be a difficult and expensive operation, but she could see," the doctor said.

"Wonderful!" Satin said. Ma looked helplessly at Pa when she came in with Caley. Caley was stroking her touchstone happily.

"The doctor says I'll be able to see, Papa," she said.

"We don't have the money, Caley," Pa said sadly.

The rest of the room was silent until Satin laughed. "Why, the doctor's my friend, Captain Priest; he and I could be your friends, if you'd let us. He wouldn't think of taking a fee from a friend."

Pa understood Fuller Satin now. We all did. "But you'd want a proof of friendship in return, wouldn't you, Mr. Satin?"

"Just keep your alien friends in check," Satin said. "For their own good."

Pa shook his head. "I don't know where you got the idea that I could control the Argans, but you're mistaken."

"Come now, Captain Priest," Satin said, frowning, "I have it on very good authority that you do have power over the aliens."

"Are you calling me a liar, Satin?" Pa's mouth grew hard.

Satin looked at Pa speculatively. "Perhaps I'm negotiating with the wrong person. Perhaps I should discuss this with your son."

There was a long awkward silence while Pa stared at me and I did my best to look right back at him.

Humming to himself, Satin sat back and looked about him. "Well," he said. "Well." And then he glanced over at Caley who had been nervously fondling her touchstone.

"What's that, Dudum?" Satin asked.

"It's a touchstone," Caley said.

"Oh?" Satin said sweetly. "May I see it?"

Reluctantly Caley passed it over into Satin's hands. Satin had at first meant to be patronizing, but the moment he felt the touchstone, his expression changed to one of awe.

"This is the most magnificent piece of Known Space sculpture that I have ever felt." Fuller Satin's hands ran delicately over the stone. He was literally almost breathless for a moment. "Where did you get it?"

"Somebody found it," Pa said carefully. "And we got it from him."

"I don't suppose you would ever think of parting with it," Satin said to Pa.

"Never!" Caley said, and she held out her hands for her stone, but still Fuller Satin would not let go of it. The stone shone as it did sometimes with a soft light so that Satin's hands looked like translucent wings.

"I'll give you a hundred credits."

"Oh, my," Ma said. She sat back with a plop in her chair.

"Inigo, sir, Mr. Satin does want that stone badly," Dudum said anxiously. "He is a friend, and it would be a nice gesture—"

But Pa cut him short. "It's not mine to sell or to give or to keep. It was given to Caley."

"And I want it," she said, and she leaned over the table, her hands reaching. Mr. Satin watched her fingers coming toward him as if they were little worms.

"All right, I won't quibble. I'll give you what it would be valued at in the imperial bazaars. A thousand credits."

Ma didn't even have the breath to say "Oh, my" this time. For once Dudum didn't have a thing to say either; he just kept on working his mouth open and shut and making little squeaking noises. But Caley had that stubborn look on her face, the way she had when she was memorizing a new room with me. She kept on leaning forward until she was almost on

111

top of the table. Her fingers found the touchstone.

"Two thousand credits," Mr. Satin said. "And forget about the aliens."

"For God's sake, Inigo," pleaded Dudum.

"It is a terrible lot of money, Inigo," Ma said.

But all Caley wanted was her touchstone. You could see it in her face, the way she kept her lips pressed bloodlessly together.

"We would like Caley's stone back, sir," I said finally. It seemed to bring back Mr. Satin and everyone from their dream.

Reluctantly Satin put the stone into Caley's hands. Caley immediately hugged it against her chest and slipped back into her chair, where she sat stroking it and feeling it as if to make sure it had not been damaged.

"It would be just like sharing between friends, Miss Priest. You wouldn't be losing it."

"It's mine," Caley said stubbornly.

Ma put her arms around Caley and held her close. "No," Caley said.

Satin looked frustrated. "It's the land, isn't it? You're mad because of the land. Well, it's yours. I'll give it to you. Just be my friends. Give me the touchstone."

There were gasps around the room, and File pushed his way forward. "For God's sake, Inigo. For all our sakes. Give him the touchstone."

And Pa's voice was gentle and quiet when he spoke. "It ain't mine to give, File. It's Caley's."

"It's too big a decision for her to make." File turned frantically to Caley. "You do want eyes, don't you?"

Caley pressed herself even tighter against Ma, frightened now. "No. No, I don't want eyes. I have Tyree for eyes. I can see right now!"

Pa hated to do it, but there were more things than just love involved in the affair. "Caley, don't fool yourself."

"No." Caley shook her head insistently. "I can see the golden towers right now and the shining people and the—"

"Are you afraid, Caley?" Satin asked. His voice was seductive and cunning. "Are you afraid that the city might not look like that?"

"Of course I know it won't look like that to *you*," Caley snapped.

"But I can see it, Caley, and it may be ugly now but I can make it look beautiful. I can make it look just the way you want it. Wouldn't it be nice to have everyone see what you see right now by yourself?"

"They can see it my way right now—if they want to, Mr. Satin." Caley said it in a quiet but dignified voice, and Satin straightened up as if he had just been slapped. The doctor tried to hide a laugh.

Dudum looked terribly pale, like he had just been tortured for three solid years. "Of course Inigo will think about it, Mr. Satin. Of course he will." And he looked to Pa for reassurance.

Caley had started to cry and that was the last thing Pa could stand. "Get out," he ordered. "Get out, all of you." He grabbed Dudum in his powerful arms and spun him around and pushed him toward the balcony. Then Pa grabbed everything from the table and shoved it into the arms of the startled Sons of Light. The Sons of Light and the doctor practically jumped off the balcony. Erasmus and Satin were the last ones down the ladder.

"The offer will stand as long as I am in the city, Captain Priest," Fuller Satin said to Pa, but he kept his eyes on Caley.

Erasmus hesitated by the balcony and began apologizing. "I just hitched a ride back here with Mr. Satin, and on the way he told me all his plans for Old Sion. Inigo, he can do so much for you."

"I'm satisfied with my life as it is now."

"But, Inigo, don't you understand why I came back so soon? Fuller Satin owns *all* of Old Sion. There was nothing left to file on."

"I figured something like that, Erasmus, but I had to try. Why don't you stay for dinner?"

Erasmus glanced over the side of the balcony. "No," he said. "Under the circumstances I can't. You'll get my resignation tomorrow, Inigo. Mr. Satin's hired me as a tutor for the children of all the Sons of—the Silkies in his employ. With this magnificent equipment." Erasmus shook his head and his voice took on a pleading note. "If you could just see the schoolroom, Inigo. It's better than anything on the mainland, even."

We understood then that it wasn't really Erasmus we were talking to, not our old Erasmus. He's been changed by money just like the others; only poor Erasmus didn't realize it yet.

Pa held up his hand kindly to Erasmus. "You better go before they leave without you."

Pa shut the doors after them like he wanted to shut out a storm and the cold, and for one moment the stars on his shoulders shone in the lights of the Commune, winking, and he looked the way Great-Great-Grandpa must have looked when he decided to leave the ships. He looked so fine in his full gear that it hurt, actually hurt, to look at him and realize this shining man was my father. And then the doors were closed and Pa was simply a man, though a little of that old glory still clung to him even when he undid his collar.

# 8
## THE RUNAWAY

WE DID NOT do much talking after Satin left. Pa did not even bother asking me about the Argans, and he cut Ma short each time she tried to ask me. It was like we could feel the whole Commune eavesdropping on us, trying to learn what we were going to do next. All of us went to bed real early—like the sooner we got to sleep, the faster we could forget about the whole day.

Only that wasn't any way for me to escape. I could hear Caley turning on her mat and every now and then murmuring "No" in a quick, hurt little voice. I couldn't sleep with her going on like that. I found my fingers moving like they were playing the flute again, so I sneaked out of the room and up the stairs to the rooftop to breathe some fresh air and maybe think things out.

But I hadn't more than got settled when I heard footsteps on the stairs: *stump, stump, stump,* up the steps, and then weighted wet boots slopping along on the old worn wood. I looked down the stairs to see the bulky figures of a boy and a man in wet suits. One of them held a small hand light. They left puddles of water wherever they had stepped.

I could see that they had already taken off their helmets and breather packs. I figured that they had walked up the street underwater so that the night watch had never noticed them, and they must have climbed into the basement which was flooded. The night watch would be too busy looking for boats or Hydra floating on the surface.

"They've gotta have it in here," Big Ham whispered harshly, "if it ain't downstairs."

"I don't like it," Little Ham said. "Those spiders—"

"In the same room with Jerusha Priest? That woman hardly lets *humans* into her house," Big Ham retorted.

I figured it would do no good to shout to Pa and I found myself wishing dearly for Great-Great-Grandpa's knife. I felt around the floor for something to use as a weapon and found Ma's bristly scrub brush. I remembered then that she had been washing the stairs that morning.

I crept down the steps cautiously until I was almost down to the fourth-floor landing. Both of them had slipped knives out of their belts and were just about to open the door into the bedroom when I jumped from the stairs. I felt my body smack satisfactorily against two pairs of legs.

Both of them fell heavily on the floor and I was on top of one before he could get up. I slammed him against the floor.

"Little Ham! Mercy on us, Little Ham!" Dudum shrieked. "They's a spider on me!" I rubbed the brush in hard and heard him shriek some more, and then for good measure I bit his arm, feeling solid flesh underneath the rubber of the wet suit. "Mercy on me, mercy! It's biting me. Get him off, Little Ham. Get him off!"

"Get him off yourself," Little Ham said. "It was your idea to come. Wouldn't be no spiders now, you said. Wouldn't be no spider fool enough to live with the Priests, you said."

Dudum was paralyzed there on the floor, too busy howling for Little Ham to help him to do anything about me, so I gave him an extra-juicy bite on his neck for good measure and then jumped for where Little Ham was talking.

Little Ham was all arms and legs for a moment, flailing and kicking out wildly, but I finally got around on his back and rode him to the floor, where I got the brush and gave his head a good polishing while I bit his hand.

"Little Ham, help me, oh, merciful God," Dudum was still yelling. He had volume and tone on Little Ham. But Little Ham had a good imagination that inspired him to wail. He jumped to his feet, tossing me off his back, and he tried to run up the steps to the roof. Dudum must have had the idea too, because the two of them collided and went rolling over on top of each other, screaming together in sheer panic.

That was how Pa found them when he came out on the landing with a moss lamp. He had a gun cradled under his arm. Little Ham and Big Ham lay in each other's arms howling to each other for help.

"Well," Pa said quietly. "Well, if it isn't the Rover Boys."

Little and Big Ham disentangled and got up slowly while I stood back, trying hard not to laugh.

"Good . . . unh . . . evening," Little Ham said sheepishly; but Big Ham stood up straight like it was normal to come into someone's house in the middle of the night.

"We were just trying to help you, neighbor."

"I see," Pa said quietly.

"We were going to see that you got the money for the stone," Big Ham said.

"Big Ham," Pa said quietly. "You may think me old-fashioned, but I still think a man has a right to say what he's going to do with his property."

"We're going to bring you into this century yet," Little Ham said.

"Hmm," Pa said and bit his lip and held the light closer to Little Ham. "Well, you'd better take care of your own back-yard first. It appears you're coming down with something, Little Ham. Your whole face is covered with little holes." With a horrified expression, Little Ham began to feel his cheek.

Pa swung the lamp over toward Big Ham. "And I wouldn't hang around with your boy for a while, Big Ham. 'Pears he's given you the same thing."

I held the brush behind me when Pa turned to me. "What do you think it is, Tyree?"

"Nothing serious," I said, trying to keep from laughing. "As long as they lie down and stay at home for the next week or so."

"But we can't—" Big Ham began.

Pa bent over and scrutinized Big Ham's tongue closely. "Lord, but it's spreading," he lied.

"Mercy on us," Little Ham said and went racing up the stairs.

"I—" Big Ham began and then snapped his jaw shut and went up the stairs just as fast as Little Ham. Pa and I bolted the roof door behind them and then we went down the stairs to where Ma and Caley crouched in a corner of the bedroom.

"What was it, Papa?" Caley asked.

"It's all right, Minnow," Pa said, putting up his gun. "Just a couple of bugs wandered into the wrong house. I don't think they'll try it again."

But Ma let go of Caley and came over to me. "Are you all right, Tyree? Your eye's bruised and your face is scraped—"

"I just lost a little skin."

"Did you have to lose it where I could see it?" Ma dragged me over toward the washbasin. "And what are you doing with my brush?"

Pa chuckled quietly. "Doing a little scrubbing, I think."

Ma had caught sight of the scene on the landing outside and figured out what had happened. "I don't think it's so funny, Inigo, when we almost get murdered in our own beds."

"Now, Jerusha, Big Ham may be a bully and a cheat," Pa said, "but he's no murderer."

"Mr. Satin won't give up, Inigo, and you know it," Ma retorted. "We'd better talk." She had us go downstairs, because one of Ma's prerequisites for thought was a cup of hot Kavo leaves. "That thing's too dangerous to keep," Ma said.

"I won't be forced to do something by any man," Pa said quietly. None of us spoke then while Ma boiled water and added the leaves to the pot. Ma began to pick nervously at her robe.

"You're all going to hate me for repeating this, but that is an awful lot of money we were offered."

"But it's my stone," Caley said. She looked as if Ma had proposed selling Caley.

All Pa would say was, "Yes, it is."

"Wouldn't you like to have eyes, Caley?" Mother said coaxingly and she tried to draw Caley against her, but Caley didn't want to be hugged.

"I don't need eyes. I can see right now. Real good. And what I can't see right away, Tyree helps me on."

"Why, Caley," Ma said. "You'd think you loved that thingamabob more than you loved your own family."

Caley turned to me, slowly, looking at me with unwinking eyes, and she was pleading silently. Her fingers ran frantically over the touchstone's surface.

"It's not fair to argue that way, ma'am," I said. "A body can love two things in two different ways but with the same strength."

Pa was a proud man and a strong one who could not understand what he took to be the defiance of his ideals— whether from the Sons of Light or from his own son. He would hold in his doubts and his anger until he was all torn up inside. I couldn't hold back my terrible secret any longer. It seemed that the longer I hesitated, the more I had to be guilty for.

"It's not disrespect, Pa. But we got a right to live our own lives on certain important things. Like, well, like me. I just had to take music lessons. . . ." And I went on telling Pa everything—about Amadeus and the lessons, the trumpet, and the Seadragon's treasure; and then about how I was going to create the Silkies' own music.

Ma twisted a towel nervously around her hand. "I just can't see how you could fool your parents, Tyree."

Pa added, "Especially when no self-respecting Silkie has time to loaf around with a flute all day."

"Great-Great-Grandpa Lamech didn't do so bad," I said.

Pa couldn't argue with tradition, so he tried a new tack.

He sighed and shifted his foot, and his boot scraping sounded like a ton of leather in that still room. "Tyree, last year it was collecting crabs and the year before that it was climbing the fronts of buildings—"

"This is different, Pa."

"That may be," Pa said, "but a man weighs his amusements against the good of his people. If you're truly sincere about your apology, you will take your flute and burn it."

There was silence in the room and I felt my cheeks burning like they used to when Pa slapped me. No one stirred in the room, not even Caley. Her fingers rested on the touchstone without moving. It felt like my insides had become china, brittling up, growing more fragile, with that tingling that passes through your hands telling you just before you break something that the glass in your hand is about to fall, a shock, and then it's broken. I was hurt and I wanted to hurt back.

"No, sir," I said.

Pa wouldn't look at me but kept tracing designs on the table. He had been pushed past a point now, by Silkies, by Satin, by me, so that he went on arguing for the sake of his hurt pride. "Tyree Priest, you will burn your flute or you are no son of mine." He looked like he regretted his words the moment he said them, but he was too proud and stubborn to take them back—as proud and stubborn as I was when I said, "Then I'm no Priest." It seemed to take an eternity to push my chair backward along the floor. I went upstairs and got my flute from the drawer where I kept it hidden. I tucked the flute through my belt when I came downstairs.

"Tyree," Caley said, and she started to come around the table, but Ma grabbed her and held her tight, telling her to hush. I didn't look at Caley or Ma—just at Pa. I took down the book of T. S. Eliot that Erasmus had given me and slipped it into my pouch, and hung that over my spear.

"Don't be a fool, Tyree." Pa nodded at my chair. "Come back here and we'll talk about it."

But I couldn't see what there was to talk about, because for the last five minutes we hadn't even been discussing anything. Pa and Ma had just laid down orders on me, which isn't much of a discussion. I just opened the door.

"Tyree," Ma said worriedly. I looked back, not at Caley—I couldn't look at her—but at Ma. It's strange to see how different a face can become in just a moment. I suddenly saw the lines and the wrinkles burned in around her eyes by too much sun and too little rest. Her silver hair was brittle and there were already streaks of white.

"Ma'am?" I asked. For her face I might have come back, but I should have known Ma better. And bless Ma, she couldn't embarrass Pa by pleading with me to stay. It was bad enough for Pa, my walking out when Pa told me not to; but it would have been twice as bad for Pa if I had stayed only because Ma asked me.

"Tyree, at least have the sense to take a little food."

"I'll manage, ma'am. Thank you." Then I was out into the night air, swinging off the balcony and down into my skiff. I kept waiting for Pa or Ma or Caley to call to me from the balcony but none of them did—none of them could. I rowed away hurriedly, feeling as if I had just killed something.

At first I didn't have any time to miss home because I was in the city, my city. I was wild with a sudden feeling of freedom, just like a bird that has broken free of its cage. The bird's wings are one blur of motion: just the way your mind feels. Nothing ever seemed more vivid and more real, and yet nothing would remain in my memory.

It was not intentional on my part, but somehow it seemed the most natural thing in the world to head for the old mansion in Sheol. I settled down on a balcony even though it was damp from the spray that continually splashed up from the street. A soft glow ran up the street from the sea worms and flowers and sea anemones opening to the wind.

I played my flute just for the hell of it at first, just to let the air escape from my lungs: for the sheer joy of having a body and a flute together at the same time without books and without parents and without anyone keeping us apart. I played some of the lively tunes Amadeus had taught me, and then some of my own things that got pretty wild, and then slipped somehow back into the more tender songs I'd learned from Amadeus. I waited patiently until late in the afternoon. I found myself listening for some sound, any sound, of Argans coming; but there was nothing. I tried looking inside the mansion.

Though I strained my eyes for a glimpse of an Argan, I saw no one until, with dust clinging to my wet legs and bits of crumbling wood and stone covering my hands, I stopped in the abandoned hall. "Amadeus!" I shouted, but all I heard were echoes of my own voice. "Amadeus!" I shouted again. I didn't even try to pretend that my flute playing would bring him now. I called to him one last time with everything inside me. "Amadeus!"

But nothing. I slumped down on the floor, feeling as if I were caught up in some nightmare, and then I heard the hiss of fur gently brushing the ceiling and the distinct popping sound of suction pads. A cloud of red eyes burned out of the darkness above me.

"Amadeus?" I asked hopefully.

"No, Manchild. I Sebastian. Amadeus send me."

I couldn't see Sebastian's body, only his eyes. I felt as if I weren't talking to Sebastian at all but to something else, strange and distant—like a faraway galaxy of red stars inhabited by some ghost.

"Come on down." I rubbed the back of my neck. "I'm getting a crick."

"I stay up here."

"But why?"

"I stay up here," Sebastian insisted.

It wasn't going to do any good arguing with Sebastian, so I went on. "I want to see Amadeus. I want to apologize to him for the other day."

"He know you don't mean it, Manchild."

"Then why didn't he come here himself?"

"Because he say it better if you no see him and he no see you anymore." Sebastian's voice was gentle but firm.

"But I'm almost like a nephew to him." I added desperately, "And I don't have anywhere to go. I left home, Sebastian."

Sebastian made clicking noises in exasperated friendliness. "You no can stay here."

"But why?"

126

"It better you not know."

I sat down stubbornly. "I'm not leaving until you give me some answers."

"Manchild." Sebastian obviously felt sorry for me. "You no want to know."

"I do."

Sebastian thought to himself for a long time. "If I tell you why you no can stay, you promise no tell anyone?"

"Of course."

Even then, Sebastian had to wait for a moment before he had enough nerve to go on. "It time for us to weave our cocoons. We need that to rejuvenate, to let our bodies become young again."

"Even Amadeus?"

"Especially Ultimate Uncle. He become young most times of any of us."

I had a sudden suspicion. "Have you just rejuvenated, Sebastian?"

Sebastian gave me a reluctant "Yes."

"Then just how old are you?"

There came another pause. "It so long . . . I have to guess . . . but I say, oh, a thousand years."

He moved over the ceiling until he reached the corner that was lit by the window. I saw that he had already rejuvenated. His fur was a midnight black and as fluffy as a newborn kitten's. I understood now why he had stayed on the ceiling. He wanted to make sure that I could not have touched him or discovered the change in him.

We were ten feet apart, but it might have been light-years. I realized then that there were some differences which music could not bridge.

"So Amadeus knew my Great-Great-Grandpa?"

"For a little while."

"Then Amadeus lied to me," I said angrily. "He told me that the other Argan was a kinsman."

"He no lie, not exactly. Rejuvenation a kind of death and rebirth. That the closest I can come to it in your Manchildren talk."

"But I still don't see why Amadeus wants me to stay away," I said. "I can guard you while you're in your cocoons. I can—"

"No, no, Manchild. That the last thing Amadeus want."

"But I thought he had forgiven me."

"He forgive you, right away. That why he no want to see you. He miss you very much after your fight and he realize that if he miss you after such little thing, that it be worse later."

"But I'll promise never to ask another question—"

"That not what he afraid of." Sebastian hesitated, so I prodded him with another question.

"Well, what *is* he afraid of?" I asked.

"He no like to see you die." There was something strained, so strained, about the emphasis placed on his last word.

Numbly, I watched him slip through the window and out into the street. A few minutes later I left the mansion, letting the current carry me out of Sheol. The deserted mansions bulked huge and squat out of the water, their roofs caved in like mouths, and the paneless windows looked like open sores on the crumbling sides; the only sounds on the silent streets were the water slowly sucking at the houses and the wind wailing through the holes.

By the late afternoon I had drifted to the northern edge of the city, to the farthest ruin in the city. It had once been the spaceport terminal. The sea had pounded three of its walls into a mound of rubble that lay under the water most of the time, so that the bricks were worn by the sea into flat, oval-shaped pink stones. But there was a fourth wall with the window niches and most of the tower intact.

I went up to the tower so I could be above everything. I felt an ache inside of me because I had left home and because Amadeus had given me the brush-off and because there were some differences between humans and Argans which could never really be ignored. And what added to the hurt was the fact that the city did not care about me and my problems—no matter how much I cared about the city. I would always be apart and separate from one of the things I loved the most.

Below me the sea anemones were tight little red knobs on the stone rubble, but as the sea rose higher and began to cover them, they opened one by one, glowing with their own inner light so that a sea of fire steadily swept toward my wall. The cool spray washed every cell of my body while I watched the creatures spread their fingers to the sea. Finally I couldn't stand it any longer. It seemed to me that the pounding of the sea became the roar of ghost rockets lost in time and space, trying to find their way home to Mother Earth. I picked up my flute and began to play. Soft, low, easy: a tune to bring the sun down and the moons up. I was alone before a vast, imponderable sea that swept on irresistibly from the horizon to rush against my wall.

And then through my misery and the sound of the sea, I heard pebbles rattling against one another. I leaned over the tower wall to see a boy about four feet from me. He was perched in the window of a crumbling wall, with one leg dangling precariously over the sill.

"Why did you stop playing?" he asked.

"I play for pleasure and for my friends," I said.

"I'll pay, Silkie," he said eagerly. I looked down at him contemptuously and decided that he was not worth insulting.

"I don't play for money."

He suddenly changed his expression. "So you're one of *those* Silkies." And from somewhere inside his suit he pulled out a camera. "Hold it."

I froze when I heard the click.

"Great." He twisted dangerously to one side of his window and snapped another picture. "Now try and smile this time." He squinted behind his camera, smiling grotesquely himself.

"I've got a better suggestion." I held up my hunting spear.

But instead of being frightened, he merely nodded. "Oh, great, great."

I twirled the spear in my hand so that the butt end was in front and hit his wrist sharply so that the camera fell out of his hand. He made a snatch at it but I had twirled the spear around so that the point was aimed right at his throat. His eyes glanced from the spear point to his tumbling camera and back to the spear point again. He swallowed uncomfortably when the camera splashed into the sea.

He reached his hand slowly towards his pants pocket. "If you want my wallet—" he began, but stopped when I thrust the spear at him.

"I don't want that."

"What do you want?" The boy was in an agony over that question. He was frightened then. Really frightened. I stared at him for a moment, realizing that what I wanted was forever out of that boy's reach, out of my reach, out of anybody's reach.

"Go on home," I said, suddenly feeling sick. "Go on back where you came from."

A rock suddenly cracked the brick by my head and I barely ducked the next one. I looked at the next window to see a girl there struggling to raise a rock as big as her head.

"Stop that," the frightened boy said. "Didn't I tell you to stay in the aircar?"

The girl indignantly set the rock down on the sill. "That's the thanks I get," she said.

I took that opportunity to leave, going down from the tower and getting into my skiff. It had been moored under me just over the mound of rubble, and I rowed it quickly away from the ruins where the boy and the girl were arguing with each other; and I tried to keep from smiling too hard. That girl was just like Caley would be, if Caley could see.

That thought sobered me. I did not like what was happening to me. What had I really done for Caley? When I had run away, I had just been thinking of myself. If I had to take account of everything I owed the Silkies and of everything they owed me, why, we'd both be the losers. They were my own kind, whether I liked it or not; I could no more leave them than I could leave myself. So I turned my skiff back toward the Silkies and home and started to row as quickly as my tired arms would let me.

I ignored the stares of the Silkies—by now the gossip about our family quarrel would have been all over the Commune. I felt as if the whole city was watching me as I rowed up the street, but I didn't let myself seem nervous. That feeling was one of those things I was going to have to live with for a while. I headed straight for home where the light was so bright from Tubal's moss. From the open windows I could hear the quiet rattle and clink of pots and Ma singing softly.

Pa was sharpening the edge of his spearhead when I came in. He flashed a smile at me and then went back to honing the edge. "Better ask your Ma to fix something quick for you, Tyree. You have to stand the first watch."

"Yes, sir," I said.

I was almost knocked over by a small, eager shape that leaped onto my back, almost choking me in hugging arms and legs. "Tyree, you came back! You came back," Caley said.

I eased her down off me. "Of course I did, Cal." I rumpled her hair affectionately, and even though Caley usually hates that, she let me this time. Then I saw the cube over in her corner.

"You kept the touchstone," I said in surprise.

Ma turned from the fireplace where she had been dishing some stew into my plate. "Folk like Satin shouldn't get their way all the time," she said grudgingly. "It'll spoil them—just like some children I know."

"Hush now," Pa said.

# 9
## STREET OF GOLD

IT WAS TIRAS Fitch's turn as lookout and he stood on tiptoe while he slowly turned the binoculars on the stand, watching for the Sunfish. He was ten and the eldest son of Javan Fitch. All we young Silkies had been sent out to the western half of the city, ostensibly to keep a watch but actually just to get rid of us until it was time for the fish run: we were too excited to sit still for very long.

The older Silkies had said nothing about my running away and Pa had ignored the whole subject—including the question of burning my flute. The younger Silkies, like Jafer, had tried to tease me. The best way to shut them up would have been to play for them but somehow I couldn't bring myself to do that. I hadn't even been able to practice since I got back. Something inside me just would not let me play songs anymore. So I did the next best thing, which was to punch anyone who tried to make jokes about my playing.

There were about thirty of us acting as lookouts in two-person shifts every hour around the clock. Every now and then we could hear the crack of rifles far away that meant the Sons of Light were killing some more predators—wild Hydra, mainly, because they annually flooded the city before each fish run. Fuller Satin was taking no chances of his guests wandering into their tentacles. For the past two weeks the city had reeked of decomposing bodies, but you got used to the smell like everything else.

We had a small fire going in a firebox on the roof so we could broil some fish. I turned the spit lazily so both sides of the fish would get cooked, while Fenya Aesir rebaited the hooks on the trap line in a slow, cautious way because she hated worms. Suddenly Tiras stiffened and clutched at the binoculars.

"They're coming," he shouted. "They're coming!" The other Silkies jumped to their feet and crowded around the binoculars. I waded through them slowly.

"Here, Tiras, let me see." Reluctantly Tiras got down and I bent over to the mount. I could see the golden cloud moving fast under the green surface of the sea. The others crowded around for a look but there was not any time for that; we had to get back to the fish run. I sent Tiras and the smaller Silkies back toward the Commune because, even rowing with the current, it would take them a longer time to travel up the street.

Then I picked up the mirror and flashed a light to the drivers. These were Silkies in boats with sheets of tin hanging over the sides, which the drivers beat to scare the fish in the direction they wanted. In the dry years, the drivers were absolutely necessary because they had to drive the fish into nets on the edge of the city. However, in the sea's years, when the city was good and flooded, the fish's path led right up the streets running north-south. The drivers made sure that most of the fish ran up the right street.

I set Jafer Purdy to undoing the binoculars from the mount while I turned toward the fish run and flashed what we had seen back to the runs. There was a tiny star of light the next moment, a small, pulsating flash from the roofs of the fish run to tell us that they had seen our signal. I looked around at the faces of the five Silkies that were left from my crew. They were my age or close to it, Pa had seen to that. For all of us it was our first time working at an important part of the run, but Pa had set us and the other inexperienced teams to drilling all through the daylight hours, and then he had had experienced Silkies tell us each evening about problems that might come up. You had to remember the next morning, because Pa or one of the other Silkies would quiz you and it meant extra exercises for you and all of your team if you forgot. For the past two weeks we could see, feel, and smell the fish runs.

We were all looking so solemn now that I had to laugh. I punched Jafer lightly in the arm and with a whoop I went down the steps, three at a time, with the others all shouting and tumbling after me. It was Joktan Aesir who caught me just as I was going through the window. He sent me straight into the street water.

I came up spluttering to find my crew already in their skiffs and ready to go join the Commune at the fish run. We were all in wet suits, so it didn't matter much how wet we got. I pulled myself into the empty spot in Joktan's skiff with his twin sister Fenya yelping all the time to be careful because she hated to get wet. For a Silkie, she could be awfully fastidious. Then the two skiffs were racing one another to the fish runs.

We came in a poor second, mainly because while Joktan rowed real hard, Fenya and I were busier splashing water on one another with our oars than we were in reaching the runs.

Pa was there by the first of the five nets which had been hung across Terran Way. He stood in the window on the east side. There were nets hung across the northern part of five intersections, and both sides of each cross street had been dammed halfway up each block to form a pen. In the fish run, for example, for Tarsus Street, the net across Terran Way would be raised so that the fish were forced left and right into the pens on either side of Tarsus Street. When both pens were filled, the nets would be raised at the mouths of Tarsus Street, shutting in the fish. The net at the intersection would then be dropped so that the rest of the fish could continue to swim up Terran Way until they met the net at the next intersection, Arimeth Street, where the whole process was repeated.

We never took more than a certain number of tons of Sunfish. Between disease, natural predators, and man, the Sunfish had a hard enough time reproducing sufficiently to match the number of deaths.

Pa smiled and leaned out the window. "Did you fall in, Tyree?"

"No, sir," I said, panting.

"Well," Pa said carefully, "you did a mighty fine imitation then. Better get something hot to drink." And when I looked ready to protest he added, "There won't be any fish at your net for an hour anyway."

On the roofs of each block were small fires in fireboxes where you could get something hot to drink and eat, and rope bridges had been strung between the roofs so you didn't need a boat to cross. Poor Caley was left to peel taro roots for the pots of stew on our block, though she tried her best not to show how bored she was. Ma dipped tin cups into the stew and gave them to us. Then Fenya, Joktan, and I sat down by Caley.

"The fish are running," Caley said. She looked excited, turning with closed eyes toward the open sea.

"Yes, I'll tell you all about them."

She beat one fist against her knee. "I wish I could see. I wish I could help."

"You could, Cal," I said quietly. Her touchstone rested against one bare foot and she reached down to the stone now with her free hand, rubbing it reassuringly.

"No," she said stubbornly.

"Then don't complain," I said surlily and finished off my stew so I could get away from there. Fenya had sat there uncomfortably, nursing her cup with both hands. She drank hers down quick when she saw that I had finished.

"That wasn't necessary," she said.

"Mind your own business," Joktan said to her and hurried her off, leaving me alone with my own thoughts. I heard the crack of rifle shots. The Sons of Light were still shooting predators. I looked up to see aircars drifting back toward Satin's ship.

I was reasonably composed when I finally joined my crew at our pen on the east side of Aficenna Avenue. Our duty would be to pull up the nets at the proper time, trapping the fish in the street. Jafer and Joktan had already taken their places in our assigned house, while the other three Silkies on my crew, led by Fenya, were at the rope on the other side of the street. I knew that the other crew of Silkies, on the west side of Aficenna Avenue across Terran Way, was just as nervous.

Jafer squatted nervously by the rope, trailing his fingers up and down the line. I sat with my legs sprawled out, tracing patterns idly in the dust on the floor, while Joktan sat in one corner.

I felt it first as a tingling through my skin. The birds and their young grew silent. There was a trembling in the air that made me shiver inside my wet suit, and a sheet of water nearly a foot high washed down our street to splash against the dam. Then we heard the Sunfish: a muted thunder from thousands of golden bodies churning the water. The sound echoed up and down the street, building steadily to a huge roar so that it was impossible to talk. The three of us found ourselves standing by the window, our bodies pressing close together for reassurance. The mirror flashed once from the rooftop, which meant that the Sunfish were being let into Tarsus Street.

All too quickly the mirror flashed twice, which meant that the Sunfish were being let into Arimeth Street. The roar swelled even louder. Joktan and I looked at one another because it should have taken longer to fill the first street. Too soon the mirror flashed for us to be ready. The pens were filling up too fast, but at the moment we were too excited to wonder about it. It was impossible to shout now, so I leaned out the window and signaled to the others across the street to be ready. Fenya waved back an acknowledgment and the three of us got ready by the rope.

The mirror flashed three times to signal that the fish were being let into our street. Flecks of foam drifted spinning into our street and the water washed even higher against the windows.

The crews on either side of Terran Way slowly raised their net until it stood taut above the water. A golden-bodied fish turned right from the net across Terran Way and into our side of Aficenna Avenue. A second fish followed. Then a steady stream of fish darted into our avenue: a cloud of gold surged against the rock dam, dissolved for a moment into thousands of gold fragments, and then tried to turn back, only to be blocked by other Sunfish trying to enter the pen.

The water churned white from the struggling fish and the air was filled with the slapping of thousands of bodies. Then Shadrach signaled with the mirror for us to draw up our nets. I waved to the crew to raise our net and then tensed by the rope as Fenya waved in acknowledgment. It had to be timed just right or the nets might break under the weight of all the fish. The net across Terran Way dropped, but the main stream of fish stupidly fought to enter the avenue, ignoring the open way.

Silently we counted to three before we pulled, the way we had been trained. My stomach muscles grew taut. We leaned far back to draw up the heavy net. It wasn't easy with all those fish pressing from both sides. Joktan was the last man on our line, and with his free hand he made sure that the rope coiled evenly at our side. I turned around and signaled to the other two to back away from the window, and slowly our net broke the surface. The water dripped down and Sunfish gleamed in the air as they leaped over the net from Terran Way, to flap down on the bodies already trapped within our pen. The main body of Sunfish slammed against the nets across our avenue, broke away in a panic and finally turned up Terran Way.

Joktan made the line fast and the three of us dropped on the floor exhausted. Jafer tried to shout something to me, but I had to mime that I could not hear. I waved Joktan down to the dam while Jafer and I climbed the stairs to the roof. I stared down at the Sunfish that filled the water from one side to the other, so many Sunfish jammed into the pen that it was impossible for them to swim.

Behind me the Sunfish continued to pour up Terran Way in a solid sheet of gold, and before me my crew were already taking up their positions. Fenya and Joktan were on the dam, kicking Sunfish back into the pen. The other two Silkies across the street manned a crane on the rooftop like Jafer and me. We stood on either side of the crane, working the crank. We dropped the sieve bucket into the pen and Sunfish spilled over its mouth. Then the two of us leaned at the crank, slowly drawing up the heavily laden bucket. The water spilled and jetted through the holes in the sieve bucket.

A hand from the third-story window below waved an okay and Jafer locked the crank into place before we swung the bucket against the window. A hook came out of the window, tilting the bucket so that the Sunfish went flapping and slithering into the room. In the room there would be trays, dollies, or small buckets in which the curing crews would haul the Sunfish into adjoining rooms on that floor that had been made waterproof, sanitized, and filled with brine. We would keep the fish in a heavy solution of brine in those rooms until they were ready for smoking or salting. The next bucket of fish went to the fourth story and the third bucket to the fifth. By that time the third story should have had a chance to clear its window and we would dump the fourth bucket through that again.

I forget how long Jafer and I were at the crane or how many times we dipped our bucket into the street. All I remember is that Joktan came up and spelled Jafer on our crane, and then it started to take longer to fill the buckets because the street was not as full. Then Jafer was hitting me on the shoulder to signal to me that it was my time to go down to the dam.

I straightened up as Jafer moved past me to take my place at the crank, and I suddenly became aware of all the aches running from my feet up to my neck. It felt so good to stretch again and ease my arms and legs. Someone pressed a cup of stew into my hands and I gulped it down hungrily. The fifth street to the north had been closed long ago and still the Sunfish kept pouring past.

And looking at all the busy Silkies, I knew that we were the people of the sea now and not of the land. It made me feel proud and yet small at the same time; it made me feel humble. And then I saw Caley, sitting lonely by the fire, feeling her touchstone nervously. There was very little she could do without eyes. I walked over to her shakily, because my legs were still weak. I tried to shout hello to her, but the noise from the sea drowned me out, so I knelt beside her and touched her lightly on the shoulder. Her face lit up and she ran her fingers lightly over my face. I could read her lips when she said my name, but that was all. I couldn't understand another thing she said because she spoke too excitedly.

I wished then that I had worked out some code with her before so that we could talk by touch. It would have been better for Caley to have stayed inside at home, but this year there were no children to keep her company; everyone was doing something on the run, and Caley refused to be left out. But it must have been horrible to be kept apart that way. Without her sense of hearing Caley was almost helpless on this unfamiliar ground. She could only sit, frustrated, unable to find out what was going on around her.

I gave her a hug. She wrinkled up her nose, making a face, and then laughed, wiping her hands down my arms. I looked down in surprise to see that I was covered from head to foot with sticky, smelly fish scales. She wiped off my cheek and very carefully kissed me there and then made motions for me to go back to work, trying to pretend she was enjoying herself. She picked up another taro root and began to peel it energetically. I left reluctantly, and when I turned at the door leading downstairs, I saw that she had put down the root and the knife and was stroking her touchstone again in her isolation. Somehow I didn't feel that being a Silkie was so great when Caley could not really be one.

The feeling stayed with me down on the dam even though I could not do much thinking about it. It was lighter work down there, but you were busy every moment. You had to kick the fish that lay flapping on top of the dam back into the pen, and also try to keep yourself from slipping off the now-slimy stones. At the same time you flailed the water with a pole soaked in repellent to drive the Sunfish to the bucket. The pole was about fifteen feet long and at the end was a sack containing a harmless but noxious mash that was made from crushing certain plants. It was a fish repellent, and wherever you put it in the water, the fish would scurry in the opposite direction.

By sunset the street was nearly empty and the Silkies with the poles were working from skiffs, driving the fish leaping before them into the buckets. That was when I went over to Caley and made her get up and put her to work on the crank. A tap on her arm would set her to cranking with all her might and another tap would make her stop, but almost busting to get back to cranking again. She did not really help much with the physical work, but it did make me feel easier, seeing her happy and working beside me.

Sometimes I would feel a shadow flitting across my face and I would look up to see an aircar full of tourists watching us, and some grinning ex-Silkie sitting back dreamlike in the pilot's seat. It hurt sometimes to see how easy they had it, especially when your back hurt and you were too tired even to raise your arms. For the most part the Sons of Light had enough sense to keep their aircars out of throwing range, or one of their immaculate tourists might have gotten dirtied by a little fish.

We worked on into the night with light provided by the street life—and moss lamps—taking short breaks to eat and maybe rest ourselves, but it was impossible to sleep because of the noise. Ma and Pa came over once, looking worried, but I signed to them that everything was okay. Then Pa came by, signaling to people it was time to grab some sleep. Ma came to fetch Caley; I saw Shadrach write something hurriedly on paper, and he and Pa went to the parapet and looked at the Sunfish with their binoculars.

The Sunfish should have tapered off by then, but they had not. There did not seem to be an end to them, but I could not see what Pa was worried about. Then Caley was tugging at my arm and I had to leave, only instead of going on home, Ma signed for me to row us on farther away from the noise and the smell. We rowed all the way to the edge of Sheol with the others, where our bedding was arranged by families.

I was tired and my ears felt almost deaf from the incessant noise, but Caley looked so fretful that I turned over on my side to face her.

"What is it, Cal?" I asked. It felt strange to hear my voice again.

Caley rubbed her stone briefly. "Nothing," she finally said. "You're tired. Go to sleep."

"I can't. Not when you look like that."

She squirmed in her blankets. "You did promise to tell me about the run."

"Caley," Ma said sternly. "It's late."

But I sat up in my blankets. "I'm not really tired, Ma," I lied; then in whispers I described what had happened that day until Caley started to breathe softly, and then I too went to sleep, to the distant roaring of the Sunfish.

The sun was just starting to rise when I felt a hand shaking my shoulder and I saw Pa crouched over me. He put a finger to his lips for me to be silent, but Caley sat up right away.

"What's going on?" she whispered.

Pa turned and sighed. "Nothing, Minnow."

Ma stirred sleepily and opened her eyes. "Inigo, what's happening?" she murmured.

Pa sat down with a quiet laugh. "Well, I thought I was going to sneak one past you people, but I guess I'm not. I figured we needed some side money so I had my own private fish run last night."

"Inigo, didn't you sleep at all last night?" Ma demanded.

"None of the men did, Jerusha." Pa looked tired but he managed to smile anyway. "There'll be plenty enough time to sleep when the winter rains come. Anyway, there isn't much left to be done now but smoke the Commune's fish we've already caught, and skeleton crews can do that."

"You have almost half the catch still to bring up from the streets," Ma protested.

"They'll stay put," Pa said. "There's enough in the streets for them to eat and we've hung repellent on the dams and the nets so they won't be jumping over." He got up slowly. "I figured that Tyree and I could take care of our own catch today."

"And me, Papa." Caley threw off her covers excitedly. "I can work the crank."

Ma frowned at me as if to say, See what comes of interfering. You should have let Caley stay put and she would not be getting these ideas. But Pa, he laughed and put his arm around Caley.

"All right, Minnow. There's no stopping a hard worker."

Ma was slightly miffed. "No, and there's no stopping some fools either," she said as she went to pack a lunch.

# 10
## SION'S WALLS

PA AND THE other Silkies had rigged up makeshift pens wherever they could find a street with some water in it. Our own private fish run was in the warehouse section right next to the spaceport terminal on the northwest edge of the city. It was a long way from Terran Way and where we had spent the night near Sheol, and the Sunfish in the streets made it hard going.

Our fish run was on a street between two warehouses, where the wall of the southern warehouse had collapsed to form a dam about a foot underwater. Some sacks of repellent had been placed on it and after the fish had been driven in, a rope had been drawn across the street some twenty feet away from the dam and sacks of repellent had been hung on the rope.

As driver, I walked along the dam, driving the fish to Pa, who drew them into the boat with a small net. When the boat was filled, Pa would row slowly over to the brick warehouse on the north side, which stood about ten feet above the water. The window ledge was only a foot above the surface, and Caley waited there for Pa to help her into the boat so they could toss the fish into metal tanks of brine. The cleaning and processing would have to come later. Caley was so solemn about the whole affair, hugging to her chest fish that seemed as big as she, but somehow I managed to keep from laughing.

We worked all that morning. It was early afternoon when an ominous rippling passed down the street, catching at seaweed and pressing it tight against the buildings. Immediately the anemones near the surface began to close and we heard the clickings of barnacles shutting on the faces of the buildings.

The boat began to ride high on the swells, and Pa turned westward to look anxiously down the street. Above the flapping of the Sunfish we heard a chilling sound: the low, keening howls, slow but rising quickly in intensity, that meant there were wild Hydra around, with small mouths on each tip of their tentacles which could tear a body apart in just a few minutes, and a beak that could punch a hole through a sheet of steel.

"Hydra," Pa whispered. He lifted Caley up out of the boat. "Pull your legs up, Caley." And she put her legs up tight against her chest so Pa could swing her through the window. "Now you get up high as you can on that roof, you hear. And don't you budge."

Then he turned to me. "Have you got your knife?" I nodded.

Pa took up his long boat hook. "You keep them off me, you hear, Tyree." I was proud and scared at the same time that he had let me stay.

"Yes, sir."

But inside my head I was thinking that it might be better for all three of us to go up on the roof. Pa picked up a little of my mood. He glanced down the street. "Whether we die now or starve to death two months from now is a moot point, Tyree. But we'll starve for sure if the Hydra get at the Commune's fish run. I'd rather stop them here by our extra catch." Pa figured that it was just one pack. If he had known how many Hydra there really were, we would have left right then.

And then you could see the hands on the parapet and Caley's head just beginning to peep over. "You stay put there now, young lady, you hear? And don't you move until I tell you."

"Yes, sir," she called down in a high, scared voice.

Hydra traveled by blowing air through a wide tube inside their bodies so that their collapsed bodies shot forward with a howl. Every now and then a tentacle would flash in the air, bright and slick, like red stalks of glass walking through green crystal.

Pa had run lines through the bolt holes at bow and stern so that we were broadside to the street and to the oncoming packs. He had made them as tight as he could, and he rose now in the stern with his muscular legs spread far apart for balance. He rested the hook against his hip.

I was sitting down in the bow holding on to the gunwale while I watched the Hydra close in. A bright-red Hydra big enough to be the granddaddy of all Hydra surfaced. It got the scent of the fish and let out a howl that nearly drove the hair from my head, and it shot forward. All the other Hydra took up the cry until the street echoed with howls.

Pa jabbed down with his boat hook and cut off that granddaddy of a Hydra right in mid-yell, lifting the Hydra for a moment out of the water. It hung like a deflated balloon from the hook; some of its tentacles slapped at the gunwale, while the others clung to the shaft. With a flick of his wrists Pa freed the hook, flinging the Hydra back toward its pack, ichor spraying a yellow line in the sea. The water frothed as the Hydra nearby smelled blood and attacked their leader, but the Hydra behind them just went right on around, jetting in toward us.

Pa stabbed down again and speared one neatly, and the moment he flung it away, he speared another and flung that back into the pack. He kept spearing them and throwing them back and more kept on coming. Some Hydra would stop for a moment to eat their wounded brother—because once the Hydra smells blood it attacks, no matter who the victim is.

Too late we realized that it was more than one pack. We were tiring fast. The muscles on Pa's back stood out and the sweat poured down his face and arms. I was cutting at the tentacles that slammed at the boat trying to grab hold of us. Once a Hydra jetted into the boat itself and landed with a sickly smack of wet flesh and lay there oozing across the floor. My knife cut through the soft flesh and the Hydra burst like an overripe fruit, mixing with the splinters my blow had chopped from the side.

Pa started to pant, and I noticed that he was swinging his arms more slowly. The Hydra had already gotten around us and you could hear the Sunfish wriggling frantically in the water and the triumphant, mad hoots of the Hydra as they jetted in for the kill. There isn't anything faster than a Hydra jetting across three yards of water. They are there one moment and the next, they are ten feet away; and before the howl has died down, they have swallowed their prey. At first there were just a few howls, but then the air was filled with hoots as the Hydra ate. By then I had to give up keeping the Hydra out of the boat and concentrate on keeping them off Pa and myself. Between kicking and cutting, I did a tolerable job, even though it was all I could do to tear them off Pa's legs with my hands. I hated to touch the things because they left a bad-smelling slime on my hands and they were slippery and cold to touch. In five minutes we were covered with little red puncture marks from their mouths, and Pa was kind of staggering.

Then the Hydra started to slam into the boat, one, two, three, *bam*—solid heavy smacks, thrusting Hydra up over the bow and stern, and the sea was alive with a sheet of restless red flesh before us and behind us.

"Cut the stern rope, Tyree," Pa said. He began to use his boat hook like a club now, clearing Hydra from the bow with each swing.

I scrambled to my knees and threw myself forward, hacking desperately at the rope until it gave. Pa dropped his boat hook then and pulled hurriedly at the lines so that we rode over the thumping, bumping Hydra to the building. Pa flung his boat hook through the window. When he saw I could not move because of the Hydra around my legs, he picked me up, Hydra and all, and lifted me through the window. Then, with a Hydra clinging to his leg, he jumped onto the sill.

I was pulling the Hydra off me, or trying to, but they clung on real tight to their meal. I yanked at their pulpy bodies until they hung out long and loose like sacks of jelly, but they wouldn't come off and kept throwing on new tentacles, as I pulled them off one by one, until finally they just hung too heavy on me, and I felt as if I were carrying stone weights from hooks sunk in my skin. I cut the Hydra bodies loose and then Pa and I pulled the tentacled mouths off.

"Well," Pa said. "Don't the two of us look a sight. Your Ma's going to give us hell, Tyree, for ruining our clothes, that's for sure." And he laughed because it was a relief just to be alive now and to have survived.

And then we could hear stone crumbling and falling into the water as Caley shouted out, "Pa, Tyree. Tyree."

We took to the stairs fast then and found Caley leaning over the parapet.

"Caley," Pa shouted and ran across the roof, but I beat him to Caley and pulled her back just before the brick under her hand fell away into the sea. Caley was all arms and tears, holding on to me, until Pa and I finally got her calmed down.

Then Pa drew her over to him and gave her a shaking. "Didn't I tell you to wait, didn't I?"

"I couldn't hear you, neither of you, anymore."

Pa gave her a quick reassuring hug. "Yes, well, we're here now."

Caley put out one hand timidly to touch Pa's chest and he winced. "You're all wet," she said in surprise. "You're wet-warm; you're bleeding."

She started crying all over again and holding on to Pa and we had to calm her again. I looked out down the street. Our boat went banging on and on against the side of the building as the Hydra swept by, and as far as I could see down the street there was nothing but red; even out beyond the street in the open sea there was a huge cloud of red.

I told Pa that I thought we could make it to the Commune if we got to the side street before the packs cut us off. Pa nodded at that and then, carrying Caley, we ran across the rooftops. I led the way, making sure each footstep was safe by tapping the spot with the boat hook before we landed on it.

When we faced the next street we went down the stairs quickly, pursued by echoes and shadows, into the darkness. The boat hook thunked the steps in rhythm until we were in a room full of light again. Pa watched while I swam across the street. The muddy water stung my cuts and I half-climbed onto the sill and waited for Caley, who swam doggedly toward my voice. When she touched the wall, she let me lift her up, her feet slipping as she tried to walk up the side of the building, and then Pa followed with the boat hook through his belt.

We climbed onto the roofs and over to the next street. "It's taking too long," Pa said, panting, as we went down the stairs. "We can't make time crossing the rooftops."

Then we heard chattering and we looked out the window to see an aircar slipping easily around the corner, close to the surface. Gribble was at the wheel, gravely lecturing a half-dozen tourists. He was coming from the northeast and flying low so I guess he hadn't seen the Hydra yet.

"Give me the knife, Tyree," Pa said. He handed the boat hook to me, diving into the water. File laughed and said something to the tourists as he slowed down the aircar. The tourists began to take pictures of Pa. Pa surfaced, squinting the water out of his eyes, swimming along easily, waiting for the aircar to come to him.

File cracked jokes about the odd animals you found in Old

Sion, like Silkies. Suddenly Pa grabbed hold of the side and swung one leg over into the aircar. The tourists screamed as Pa slipped my knife from his belt.

"What kind of joke is this, Inigo?" File turned around, annoyed.

"No joke," Pa said. "The Hydra are running."

"Hydra?" File went pale.

"Packs of them," Pa went on grimly. "And you're going to take me and my children back to the Commune."

"Take us to the ship," a tourist demanded.

"First to the Commune."

"I got my passengers to think of," File said angrily to Pa. He nodded his head back toward the people. "First I gotta get them to safety."

"You can warn your ship by radio," Pa said. "Your tourists are in more danger from me right now than they are from the Hydra."

For one moment it looked like File was going to try to call Pa's bluff, but in the end he turned and saw me and Caley standing by the window. He swore softly, swinging the aircar back toward the window. I hooked the side with the boat hook and eased it in. Caley climbed down like a real lady.

"You ought to have more sense, Inigo," File said quietly. He swung the aircar away and we huddled up against one side with Pa while File took us quickly through the streets. The howling was distinct now and the Mainlanders began to crouch in the opposite side.

It was my first ride ever in an aircar. The city swept by dizzyingly and File glanced grimly over toward the red street and then back to Pa. He left us on the edge of the Commune and shot away from the roof, nearly bowling us over in his backwash.

Ma pushed her way through the startled Silkies. "Inigo, where were you?"

Pa straightened up, trying not to look tired. "I'm all right, Jerusha."

"All right; well, just look at you," Ma scolded him. Our wet suits hung now in rubbery strips, and Pa and I were bleeding from a dozen places.

"I'm all right," Pa said, annoyed. "Did everyone get back?"

"If you're asking whether everyone else had enough sense to come back," Ma snapped impatiently, "the answer is yes." Pa winced a little as Ma unzipped his wet suit, because it touched some cuts.

"Then what we have to do—" Pa tried to turn around to Shadrach but Ma pulled him back to face her.

"Is to get some bandages on the two of you," Ma said. "You can give your orders just as well through Shadrach and Tubal as you can yourself."

Pa winked at me. "We don't seem to have much choice about taking it easy, Tyree, for all of ten luxurious moments. How much time do we have to get ready, Tubal?"

"Maybe an hour, Captain," Tubal said. "The howling's farther away now."

"Well, at least all that trouble got us an hour extra." Pa sighed.

He started to give orders then to Shadrach and Tubal, interspersed with orders from Ma to stand still and to turn this way or that. Fenya was even worse than Ma as she bandaged me up, because not only did she order me around but she had to throw in side questions too, like how did I ever get a cut *there*, until it was the hardest thing to keep from bandaging her mouth.

The Silkies all crowded around Pa looking anxious, and even though Pa was tired and worried himself, he could not let it show. He looked confidently at everyone and then smiled delightedly. "Afternoon, Erasmus."

Erasmus self-consciously held a pole to which a knife had been lashed as a makeshift spear. He was wearing the same old suit I'd seen for thirteen years, not the one Satin had given him. He'd made a Son of Light bring him here as soon as he'd heard about the Hydra. "I'm glad to see you're all right, Captain."

"I feel the same way, Erasmus," Pa said. "You're the educated man. Tell me why there are so many more Hydra than normal."

Erasmus shook his head sadly. "I warned Satin, Captain, but he wouldn't listen. Maybe you noticed the extra Sunfish that passed through the city?"

"It was hard not to."

Erasmus adjusted his glasses uncomfortably. We could tell he did not like being the center of attention. "That was because the Sons of Light had been killing off all the natural predators, like the Hydra, that usually eat part of the Sunfish population." He spoke slowly, glancing around at the group. "When they killed off the natural predators, they created a vacuum in the city. All these new Hydra are fighting with one another to take over the new territory. If there were time, we could just sit back and let them fight it out among themselves for the city until eventually the population of Hydra would be about normal."

"If there were time," Pa said.

"Isn't there anything else we can do?" Benteen Heth asked.

"The Hydra are too stupid to know a bad smell like repellent," Pa said. "And I've seen them go on land for food, so not even our caches are safe from them. Now I figure it this way. We'll only have a chance to make one stand. Either we can fight for just the caches by defending the houses, or we can fight for both the streets and the caches by defending the dams."

Mash Purdy stepped in front of Pa then. "But we need both to feed the whole Commune."

"That's right," Pa said quietly. "But if we save the caches, at least a few families can stay on."

"But that will be the end of the Silkies," Erasmus protested.

"Well." Pa smiled slightly. "All good things must come to an end. Now what will it be? The caches or the whole Commune?"

For a long time everyone was silent while they thought about what Pa had said. Then Shadrach coughed. "Speaking for myself, I say fight for the whole thing."

"Even if it'll be easier defending just the caches?"

"I figure we either stand together or we fall together," Shadrach said, and the others either grunted or nodded their approval.

Pa grinned broadly. "That was in my mind too."

Suddenly Purdy threw down his spear, disgusted. "Why fight at all?"

"Why didn't you go with the Sons of Light, Purdy?" Pa asked patiently.

"Because I wouldn't let no man force me out of my home without a fight."

Pa nodded. "I won't walk away from something that I and my fathers have worked for all our lives and let anyone, be it man or animal, just come on and take what he wants. But I wouldn't hold it against any man if he was to take his family over to Satin."

"And live off Satin's bread, no." Mash Purdy picked up his spear.

Pa sighed. "Then everyone to his post and God help us all."

"Amen," Ma said as she went on bandaging up Pa.

# 11
## "SIMPLE GIFTS"

I FELT LIKE I was trapped in an armor of bandages as I walked stiffly down the stairs. Pa had already gone on ahead to see to the storing away of food caches all around the city. I settled down on the dam with Erasmus and Jara Genteel; all of us wore diving suits rather than the thinner wet suits because it would take even a Hydra a longer time to bite through the tough fibers.

Since the Hydra were all on the west side, Pa figured that they would try to come straight over the dams on the western half of the fish run, so he had set us up accordingly. The men and women in the skiffs pulled up in position before the dams after they had finished caching away our emergency supplies. On each street, the skiffs would be our first line of defense. Children and old men and women were in the buildings on either side of the street, ready to pull the skiffs in against the houses. There were four skiffs ahead of us, each with a spearman and a steersman. The second defense line was formed by three of us on the dam and a reserve in two skiffs behind the dam to reinforce the wall if necessary.

The small children that were posted as lookouts began to

shout shrilly from the rooftops. "The Hydra!" they yelled. "The Hydra's coming!"

The spearmen tensed in their boats, resting their spears across their knees in readiness while the steersmen unsheathed their knives and made sure of the lines leading to the houses. The howls echoed up and down the street and the spearmen rose carefully, raising their spears by their hips. I stamped my feet nervously, hating all the delay. There was a guide rope strung at about waist level across the dam and I tried leaning against it with my belly while I jabbed experimentally with my spear. The spear felt too slick in my hands and I wiped them for the tenth time on my suit.

Then the men in the skiffs started to spear Hydra frantically. But as fast as the spearmen killed, some Hydra still got through to the dam. Erasmus got the first one with an expert thrust. It wrapped itself around his spear, the tentacles entwining about the shaft. Erasmus grinned self-consciously at his students, shook the Hydra off his spear, and then turned back to watch for others.

The boats rocked madly in the water and foam went swirling around them, and it was all the steersmen could do to keep the skiffs from overturning even as the Hydra crawled into the skiffs. As fast as spear and knife could clear the sides, there were more animals trying to get at them, until by sheer weight the animals forced the skiffs back, whirling at first and then yawing back and forth on their mooring ropes as the crews in the houses pulled the boats in.

Now it was up to us on the dam to stop the Hydra. Tentacles suddenly swung before me and I thrust sharply at a Hydra, sweeping it out of the water and tossing it back to the others. There was a slapping sound at my ankle as a Hydra grabbed it, and Jara rushed in hanging dangerously on the guide rope as she touched the Hydra with her stun stick. The Hydra howled and there was the smell of burning flesh and it jerked back, its tentacles coiling into tight balls. It slipped with a resounding splash back into the sea. The Hydra gathered howling in the street to watch us with dark eyes. Suddenly ten of them flung themselves at the dam simultaneously.

A spear darted into a Hydra beside me and I grinned my thanks to Fenya. With the butt end of my spear I swept two Hydra back into the sea. Jara had rushed at a Hydra on her left even as tentacles whipped out of the water and around her ankles. She let out a yell and dropped her stun stick to grab hold of the guide rope, even as the Hydra pulled her off the dam.

She held on to the guide rope grimly as the Hydra swarmed up her body. Then Erasmus and I were there. I pounded down the dam, jumping over a Hydra in the way, and landed by Jara. Erasmus had dropped his spear and was pulling Jara out of the water, the lower half of her body lost in a mass of Hydra. Fenya stood up in her boat, grabbed hold of the rope, and pulled herself onto the catwalk, knocking Hydra away from Erasmus with her spear. I grabbed hold of Jara's other arm and helped pull her out of the water. Jafer joined me on the dam, and his spear was a blur as he beat back the Hydra.

Jara may have been small and young but she was not weak. Later we learned that she had lost a quart of blood in the first few moments of being surrounded by Hydra, but she still managed to get to her feet. With my knife I carefully cut one Hydra in half and it dropped off Jara onto the dam. Both halves oozed toward me. I leaned against the guide rope, kicking one half into the sea and the other half into the street.

Then the boat crews behind us came onto the dam and there were a dozen spears fending off the Hydra. The whole thing seems like a mad nightmare now, but mercifully I was not thinking at that time; I kept on killing in a set rhythm like some butchering machine, stabbing with the spear in my right hand, chopping with the knife in my left.

The air was filled with the smell of sizzling flesh and it reeked of blood; and still down the street I could see more red shapes, an endless stream of them. Half of a Hydra tried to climb the wall again and I thrust it back into the tentacle-mouths of another Hydra that tore it apart in seconds.

But there were too many of them and too few of us, and one by one we had to be pulled in boats to the houses, and each time one of us fell, it was harder for the rest of us to fight off the Hydra. Our strokes became less sure and more difficult with each swing, until eventually it seemed that there were as many Hydra behind us as there were in front of us and the dam was covered with red Hydra.

Fenya jumped into a boat. "Tyree, come on," she shouted. Shadrach Lawson flung himself into the boat along with another man. I jumped into the water and grabbed hold of the stern of the boat.

"Pull," Shadrach shouted and the three of them tugged at the rope while the house crew pulled at the same time. We slid and bumped our way over the live, wriggling Hydra. I held on grimly to the sides of the boat even though my body seemed encased in tight, red-hot rings. When we reached the house,

Shadrach took one of the extra ropes dangling from the window and tied it under my arms.

"Take him up fast," he shouted, and the crew in the house pulled me up out of the water. I looked down to see myself wrapped in layer upon layer of wriggling animals. Their mass alone must have doubled my weight. I could hear the crew above grunting as they pulled me up against the wall, scraping indignant Hydra off me. The three in the boat pulled and chopped at the Hydra even though they themselves were in danger of tipping over. With my left hand I felt at my belt, found my knife and began chopping clumsily at the animals on my chest.

"Watch it," Fenya said, ducking. She forced the knife out of my fingers and began shaving Hydra off me until suddenly I felt free of the cold, moist flesh: I could feel the air cool on my body. I was jerked up and over the sill roughly and the other three quickly climbed in the window, kicking free of the Hydra that had managed to fill the boat while they had been freeing me.

Inside, Fenya sheathed my knife for me. "We are going to run out of bandages trying to cover you, do you realize that? You're a Priest all right." She shook her head affectionately and set to work with the others to pull off the tentacles that still clung to my legs.

Old Grandpa Aesir was by the window with a pole, knocking the Hydra back. "We'll have to get up to the roof," he said and casually smashed one Hydra that I had brought in with me.

"I can walk," I said stubbornly. Fenya and Shadrach helped me to my feet and I stumbled forward to the stairs. My diving suit had dissolved into shreds that hung from my neck, and I was covered with welts and cuts, but nothing serious. It looked much worse, I suppose, than it actually felt, because Fenya followed me anxiously up to the roof.

Ma was up there, bandaging another Silkie. The moment I set foot on the rooftop, Fenya grabbed hold of me. "All right," she said, "you proved yourself. Now sit down."

"You're not in such great shape yourself." I pointed to her arm.

She laughed. "We'll bandage each other."

Grandpa Aesir was the last one up the stairs and he slammed the door shut behind him. "There's no going back that way," he declared. Because of the howling from the street, we could barely hear the distinctive chorus of popping sounds Hydra make when they travel on the land. The suction power of a Hydra's tentacles is really strong, so that they can pull themselves along, moving jerkily like some kind of ten-legged bug. The Hydra reach out a couple of tentacles, get a grip, and start to pull themselves along while they extend a couple more tentacles to get a grip farther on.

Grandpa Aesir stamped to the edge of the roof and looked down. "The devils are still coming into the house. It won't be long before they'll be after us again."

We all sat silently, working at our wounds, while the Hydra thumped around below, gobbling up the cache in the house. There was not much hope that they would go away because Hydra could stay out of water for as much as half a day. In an hour's time, they had climbed the stairs and begun to thump against the door to the roof.

Shadrach took charge then. Pa had caused ropes or rope

bridges to be hung over strategic streets. We crossed the rooftops to the next street, which was clear of Hydra. Shadrach and the others who could use both arms crossed the rope bridge first and then the children went across. Then those who could not walk were lifted across the street on slings, and finally those of us who could danced along the bridge, each holding on tightly with his one good hand. Across the way, the door crashed outward and Hydra spilled onto the roof we had abandoned.

"We'll be safe here for a bit," Shadrach said. "We'll wait here for someone to find us." It was a relief to be free from the Hydra, but at the same time you could not help but start to look toward where the rest of your family had been stationed. Shadrach took up a count of how many weapons we had left and there were pitifully few.

"There's someone coming," Fenya shouted. Pa strode across the rooftops anxiously with Caley's arms wrapped around his neck and her legs about his waist. He kissed Ma hello and gave Caley to her. "Hello, Tyree," he said.

"We couldn't hold them back, sir," I said.

"No," Pa said. "But you held the longest of any of us." He looked around ruefully. "And it looks like you got cut up the most." He turned to Shadrach then. "I've signaled to everyone to move north. We'll rendezvous at the place where we slept last night. It's too dangerous in the south, even in the Commune."

He let down a sack from his shoulder and gave it to Ma. "I got what I could from home before the Hydra got there."

Ma took the sack and looked in. "Inigo," she said in exasperation.

Pa shrugged good-naturedly. "They're the necessities, Jerusha."

Ma let the sack go. "Your Captain's cap and Caley's touchstone and Tyree's flute? Why, there are only three pieces of dried fish here."

"Oh, now, Jerusha." Pa gathered up both Ma and the sack in one arm. "What does it matter if the stomach's empty as long as the soul is filled."

"Well." Ma sniffed. "Don't you go blaming me a week from now when I have to make a stew out of your boots."

Pa had managed to save some of the skiffs, and these took our badly wounded. Some of the skiffs contained men with stun sticks and spears to escort the wounded. The rest of us were to make the trek across the rooftops to the rendezvous point when the moons rose.

The Hydra had just about stripped the streets clean of any luminescent life, and for the first time I had ever known we were in complete darkness. I held on to myself tightly to make sure that I was still there as the darkness slowly dissolved my body before my eyes. The stars grew more distinct but they gave no light, and they and the lights from Satin's ship merged into one flat background of tiny lamps.

"What was that?" Caley asked breathlessly. Her voice came disembodied from the dark.

"What was what, hon?" I heard Ma ask.

"A Hydra, to the right," Caley said.

A yell came a moment later, and the sound of a spear thunking solidly into the roof.

"Everybody come in toward my voice," Pa called out.

From all over the rooftop we could hear the Silkies shuffling and crawling over to Pa until we felt them jammed in tight about us.

"Folk with weapons to the outside," Pa said, and I slowly pressed my way through the bodies until there was no one left in front of me.

"Ah," Purdy grunted painfully and I heard the soft sucking of a wet body suddenly lifted up from the roof, followed by the chopping sound of a blade on the rooftop.

"Captain," Fitch said, "there's nearly a half hour to moonrise and we can't last much longer like this. Not if we don't know where the Hydra are."

"Well, I won't have us breaking our necks on those rooftops either," Pa said.

And then I heard Caley's voice. "But Papa, *I* know where the Hydra are. I can hear them."

Pa was desperate enough to try anything once. "You Silkies on the outside," he told us, "call out your names so Caley will know where you are."

Almost immediately after we had finished calling out our names Caley shouted, "There's one by Mr. Lawson right now."

I strained my ears, and I thought I heard the softest of plops but I could not be sure. Lawson's spear tapped at the roof until suddenly there came a howl that was twisted off at the end as Lawson killed the Hydra. "And by Jafer," Caley said.

The butt end of Jafer's spear rasped across the concrete until we could all hear the hissing as he knocked the air out of the Hydra. Two sharp clinks marked Jafer's two thrusts. We stood a little bit more at ease then, depending solely on

Caley's small, childish voice for guidance to strike out at the darkness. She was never wrong once and she kept on calling out Hydra even when the first moon had risen over the city.

"All right, Caley," Pa said. "We can see now."

Flushed with her success, Caley demanded, "Is everyone all right?"

"Thanks to you, hon." Ma tried to give her a kiss but Caley shook free.

"I told you," she announced gravely, "that I had eyes."

"Well, there's a place under the sun for every person, I guess," Pa said and gave her shoulder an affectionate squeeze before he turned to give instructions.

It was a sad enough procession of Silkies that traveled across the rooftops, trying to ignore the hoots of the Hydra below. It was not easy to lose our fish caches, knowing that without them we would have to leave the city. Groups of people kept straggling in for an hour, spreading out over a square block of rooftops. When we finally could take a head count, we found that the Commune had lost ten Silkies in the fight with the Hydra, and almost all of the rest of us were wounded in some way. The fact that the entire battle had been futile only added to our sense of frustration.

Pa had managed to cache some of the Sunfish, tanks of water, and blankets at various spots that had looked like potential rendezvous points. Pa and Shadrach and some of the other men fetched the fish and blankets from the other sites and brought them back to where we were now. We all knew that there wasn't enough saved to feed the whole Commune for a winter. We lay or sat scattered over the rooftops, too exhausted and beaten to talk. The only sound besides the Hydra were a few babies crying, and maybe every now and then somebody drank cool, fresh, sweet water from the tanks Pa had stored.

After the wild confusion of the fight, the rooftops seemed strangely peaceful—with the howling Hydra distant and remote in the streets below—no tentacles, no gaping beaks, just the feeling of freedom with the unbroken sweep of roofs all about you. The only ugly sight was Satin's ship staining the rooftops with its shadow.

A single aircar disengaged itself from Satin's ship to drift slowly over the city. Shadrach swore quietly. "A lot of good they did us."

"Quiet," Pa said in a tired voice, but Shadrach was too tired and too bitter. He went right on swearing at Satin and the Sons of Light.

"Quiet," Pa said.

Shadrach then suggested that they throw a couple of boat-loads of Hydra into the ship and see who won. Benteen agreed with the sentiment but he allowed as how some tourist would be the first to find the Hydra and probably eat *them* all up as some new delicacy.

That was when Pa struggled to his feet. He swayed a little back and forth because he had just conducted one fish run, fought two battles with the Hydra, and led his Silkies to safety—and all this without any sleep and with hardly a thing to eat. "Be quiet!" he shouted.

The Silkies all looked toward Pa and he stood there for a moment, trying to blink back the exhaustion, trying to find something inspirational to say, but in his heart he knew we had lost the city and everything else that had gone with Silkie life. Then he turned to me.

"Tyree."

"Sir?"

"Play something, Tyree." And Pa lowered himself down onto the roof.

I took out my flute, too tired to be self-conscious.

"What shall I play, sir?"

"Anything. No." Pa shook his head groggily. "Play 'Sweetwater.' "

The night was a sultry one when the slightest movement brought beads of sweat instantly to your skin. The smell of still water mingled with the stench of decomposing flesh. I dragged the hot, dull air into my lungs, breathed in the smell of dead fish and carrion, old brick and stone; breathed in with tired chest muscles until my lungs could hold no more, and then I began to play, soft at first, until I surprised even myself at the sound.

The Silkies began to sit up all over on the rooftops, listening to the notes of the new song. Then someone realized you could sing the old "Sweetwater" lyrics to the new tune and they began to do just that. On that hottest of nights I could hear Ma and Pa beginning to sing the words softly: like the sound of a fresh rainfall, drops that ran liquidly, quickly, and quietly from the roofs onto the ground, fusing into a stream, a soft creek in a shadowed valley of woods that poured on down to the sea. The old Anglic when translated into Intergal meant:

Come to the sweet water,
Cool water, well water;

By the well a cedar bucket,
Dip the gourd into the water . . .

Taste the water, cool water,
Sweet water, promised water.

"Oh," Caley said beside me. "Oh." And Caley stood and turned slowly, her hand holding up the hem of her skirt, showing her slender legs as they moved in a stately and measured pace. Her little girl's face was unbelievably serene and grave—a peaceful look—as her feet danced slowly over the roof, one hand waving gracefully in time to the music of the sea.

We sang and played some other songs, but those do not seem as important as that first one. I remember even now the moment when I put down the flute to find that the other Silkies had been singing, even Tubal with his deep bass. Pa leaned over then. "I guess," he said to me, "that there's a use for music after all, Tyree."

# 12
## THE SEADRAGON

ABOUT MIDNIGHT THE small planktonic animals started to come into the city, washing in slowly with the sea swells to replace those that the Hydra and Sunfish had devoured. Fine little pinpricks of light filled the black crystalline sea like stars in a night sky, only sharper. I stood on the parapet watching the black liquid night rise and fall in the city, dissolving brick and stone, feeling as lonely and proud as our ancestors must have felt when they first went into space.

Maybe the Silkies were meant to lose the city; maybe we were meant to be a homeless people, restless as the universe we wandered through. Faint wisps of smoke rose from the watch fires, dipping and dancing in the soft breeze before they disappeared. A single Hydra let out a howl that echoed through the street and a stir passed through the sleeping Silkies, but the Silkies on watch went right on pacing, all of us looking so small above that vast sea and beneath that immense sky—like little toys on tiny concrete rafts, floating gently away into the night to be lost forever.

Pa unrolled himself from his blanket, stretching quietly and trying to rub the feeling of the hard roof out of his back.

He glanced at my empty blanket and then at me silhouetted against the parapet. He shuffled over, rubbing the aches out of his bandaged legs. "Your Ma's still not sure if she can make a tolerable breakfast."

"Yes, sir," I said and waited until Pa had eased himself down onto the parapet, resting on his elbows, before I asked him, "Sir, what will we do?"

Pa cocked his head casually to one side. "Don't know about you, Tyree, but I feel like traveling south a little. I expect Jubal will take us in for a while. He told me that there's a big archaeological dig down there. I expect I can get work."

"I'd like that," I said, and companionably we looked out together over the dying city. "But what about the other families, sir? The Silkies can't all go to Jubal Hatcher."

Pa shrugged like it did not matter to him. "The other families are going to take berths in the fishing fleet. The companies let the families stay on the processing ships now. None of them want to chance the mainland anymore."

"Except us," I said.

Pa nodded. "Except us." I looked out at the dark streets, in a turmoil over whether I wanted to leave or not. Then a huge bellow came out of the dark sea, echoing up and down the streets.

"Seadragon." Pa gripped the parapet tightly. "But she's never been this close before." Blankets fluttered all around the rooftops as Silkies got up hurriedly.

Erasmus shambled over to us, blinking the sleep from his eyes. "She must be curious about all the noise."

Suddenly a sheet of water ten feet above tide level went racing down the street, washing into windows and tossing the

174

boats up sharply to slam against the houses. A can rattled on the parapet and splashed into the sea, and the wash of water swept in suddenly through the windows below, banging doors inside. The water subsided a little and left the boats parallel to the highest story, the water spilling with each swell through the windows.

"There!" Pa pointed to the south where a huge black spot moved over the liquid night so that the phosphorescent animals flowed in its wake in a solid track of color.

"What is it? What is it?" Caley insisted.

Slowly a shadow passed before the stars and sky: a silhouette of a head rising in the night, her eyes gleaming like twin moons floating over the water. The animals in the sea danced about her neck or were sucked in to cling to her skin like a shining gold collar of light.

Ma's hands tightened protectively around Caley. "Seadragon."

"I've never seen anything so big . . ." Pa said, almost in awe.

She moved forward, the eyes unwinking. We huddled closer together. Pa put his spear down on the rooftop.

"We'll have no need of this, one way or the other," he said. His voice was strong and quiet. "If she finds us, she finds us. There's no fighting that thing."

We watched breathlessly as the Seadragon swam slowly about before the city. The swells rode up the street higher and higher, and the windows on the highest stories crashed in and the water surged into the houses. The silhouette drifted across the sea, serene, tranquil, inviolable, like the tall silent towers of the ruined city.

She squeezed among the warehouses and the swells swept higher. A warehouse fell and the Seadragon, frightened at the roar of falling masonry, lashed her tail, destroying more of the warehouses. She lifted her head, startled, as houses crashed all about her. Rubble piled up on her back, robbing her hide of its slick wetness. She moved forward cautiously. A cloud of dust momentarily obscured the beast until her frightened head reared out of the darkness. Pa slipped his arms around us, not for protection, but for a feeling of closeness.

"What's happening, what's happening?" Caley asked.

"She's coming," I told her. "But she's so big that she's breaking the buildings." There came a roar that subsided into a rumble. "A house just fell," I told her, and the debris piled up on either side, sliding away behind the Seadragon into the sea.

"Will she come here?" Caley asked Pa.

"I don't know, honey."

Rock crumbled into the sea with a hiss, leaving twisted beams of steel like bent reeds. The sea rose almost to the roof and Pa involuntarily drew us back.

"The water." Caley clutched at her hem, frightened.

"Easy, sweetheart, easy." Pa soothed her. It must have been horrible not to be able to see, but only to wait. I was too awed by the Seadragon to speak, too afraid even to whisper before that huge presence.

The great triangular head of the Seadragon hovered over the city as if the houses were part of a puppet's cardboard background. We held tighter to one another. She paused before our street like a machine of smooth, oiled muscle, encased in leather. I felt like I was standing under a huge boulder that was about to fall and there was nothing I could do but watch it.

She swung her head around as if to take her bearings and the plankton in her wrinkles flickered and glistened. Her eyes fixed on the one and only thing big enough to interest her: Satin's ship, which was lit up almost as bright as day. In fact it was so bright that you could hardly see the stars when you were near it. The Seadragon turned down the street, away from us.

"She's turning," Ma told Caley joyfully. "She's turning."

"Right toward Satin," Pa said solemnly.

The long, serpentine body flowed around the corner, sending wave after wave rolling toward us to crash against the parapet, the spray washing us like rain. Hydra ran hooting and screaming in the water, trying to climb out of the water onto the buildings until the wake of the Seadragon brushed them away, sucking them back into the water that surged around her tail.

Aircars swept out in a steady stream from Satin's ship. All you could see were their flying lights. They swirled around the Seadragon's head like fireflies. Their guns popped steadily in the distance, but the Seadragon was drawn on by Satin's ship. A high-pitched whine floated across the city.

"They're trying to rev up the engines," Pa said, but Satin's ship had an awful lot of mass and it took time to build up enough energy to send it up in the sky.

"Why don't they turn off their lights?" Pa asked help-lessly. The aircars swept in now; their lights winked out as they crashed against the Seadragon. The scream of tortured metal floated out to us distantly, a remote sound, as if it were happening in another world altogether. The aircars threw themselves in waves at the Seadragon in a vain attempt to stop her. The Seadragon would stop for a few seconds and shake herself, sometimes snapping at the annoying cloud of aircars, but she always kept on.

"Can't anybody say that the Sons of Light were cowards now," Pa said quietly, because in just a few minutes only half the aircars were left. Then Satin's ship began to rise, painfully slowly. The Seadragon hesitated before the boiling water, craning her neck to the side to take a better look at the ship. A line of aircars swept in to rattle all along her neck and she turned angrily, her jaws crashing like huge bronze gates. With a scream Satin's ship flew up from the city. The Seadragon strained after the ship, but it slipped to the side and away. The ship hovered five hundred feet above the ruins, waiting to take in the surviving aircars.

The Seadragon swung her head around, ignoring the houses she was crashing against. She turned south down Terran Way. We watched in silence as the buildings around the fish run fell. It was small consolation to us to know that we would have lost our fish caches to the Seadragon anyway, even if we had been able to hold off the Hydra—especially when the Seadragon turned west toward the Commune.

"Oh, Inigo," Ma said. "What will we do if she goes in there?"

"We just lose it a few months sooner. That's all," Pa said.

"Lose what?" Caley asked.

"Our homes."

"Oh," Caley said in a small voice. "But where will we live?"

"Hush, Caley," Ma said.

"You never tell me anything. What's happening now? What?" clamored Caley.

The monster surged forward. A woman, Mrs. Purdy, screamed. The Kahns' greenhouses collapsed like empty shells—the panes so painstakingly wired and soldered together and the heavy beams scavenged from all over the city—all lost with a roar and tinkling like myriads of crystalline bells.

Then she turned northeast again, toward us.

Caley panicked for the first time. "I can hear her breathing." She squirmed around in Ma's arms, frightened, turning her head from side to side, growing more tense with each passing second.

"What does it look like, Mama? What?"

"Like a Seadragon, honey. We've told you what she looks like."

"No," Caley insisted. "The other noise."

A familiar head appeared over the parapet, a very wet, disgruntled head. A head that had been gray but was now black.

"Amadeus?" I said in surprise. "What are you doing here?"

Amadeus looked at me, amused, with half-open eyes. "What does it look like I'm doing? I'm succoring the weak and the helpless, what else?" He put two wide hand-feet over the parapet and pulled himself over, dropping onto the roof with a wet *plop*. "Look at this," he grumbled. He gestured toward his matted fur. "Barely out of the cocoon and already ruined."

"You look handsome, Amadeus," I said, and he did, with the new coal-black fur bristling up and down his arms. My admiration made him feel a little better and he set to trying to wipe the water from his face at least.

"Get away while you can, sir," Pa said to Amadeus.

"What?" Amadeus said indignantly. "And let a promising young musician get trampled underfoot by a Seadragon? I should say not; and besides," he added, "the Seadragon got me wet."

"Amadeus, you heard me?" I asked.

" 'Course I did. Wherever there's some music in this city, that's where I am. You don't play half bad for a Manchild. Now give me the egg and I'll lead that Seadragon away from here."

"You mean the Seadragon's treasure is an egg?" I asked. "But the egg's so small, compared to the Seadragon."

"I heard that on Earth hundred-foot squid start out no bigger than the head of a pin," Pa said. "So do humans, for that matter."

"So if you'll just give me the egg, little lady," Amadeus said.

But Caley held her touchstone closer to herself. "No. Not that."

"Caley, you give the stone to Mr. Amadeus right now." Ma shook Caley, but she only held on to the touchstone even more stubbornly. Ma looked over at Pa. "Make her give it up, Inigo."

"It's Caley's," Pa said then. "To do with as she wants."

A swell of water spilled over the parapet, splashing around our feet, and Caley shifted a little, pressing the touchstone against her cheek like she wanted to force it into her body. Ma dropped her hands away and Caley turned toward me.

"It's mine, isn't it, Tyree?"

"That's right, Caley."

"It's all I got that's valuable. It's worth two thousand credits."

I could have told her that her family was more precious than any animal, vegetable, or mineral, but that would have been emotional blackmail and I wouldn't stoop that low.

"It is very valuable, Cal," I agreed.

We waited, breathless, on the rooftop while the Seadragon moved inexorably toward us. Once again Caley was responsible for our safety. She bit her lip and her face flushed as she realized that. Caley ran her fingers lightly over the touchstone and then thrust it impulsively toward Amadeus. "Oh, all right. There."

Amadeus snatched it from her hands while Ma gathered up Caley and hugged her tight. Amadeus pursed his lips together and let loose a series of chilling, shrill whistles until the touchstone began to glow.

Caley said with wonder, "I can almost see it."

Amadeus's whistles went beyond the range of my hearing, though I could feel a tingling sensation in my skin. The light from the touchstone grew brighter and brighter until Amadeus's hands became as translucent as smoked glass and the new fur about his face shone with fine diamondlike tips.

A nephew appeared across the street, waving his hands impatiently, but Amadeus held out the touchstone understandingly to Caley. She ran her fingers briefly over her stone one last time. "It's alive," she said breathlessly. *"I always knew it was alive."* Then reluctantly she brought her hands down by her sides. Amadeus whirled and threw the touchstone across the street. It tumbled shining through the air and his nephew leaned forward from the parapet and caught it easily. He immediately ran across the rooftop to the side of the street perpendicular to ours. He plunged into the water, swimming with six arm-legs, while the other two held the touchstone above his head. The light from the stone rippled across the water as he clambered up the other side, his fur bristling, and handed it to the next Argan.

"That would have to be Sebastian." Amadeus shook his head. "He's liable to do anything when he gets excited."

We watched the stone travel on down the street, sometimes tossed over the water, sometimes passed excitedly from hand to hand until the carriers were lost in the darkness and all you could see was the touchstone gleaming like a star in the night. I made sure to tell all this to Caley just as it happened.

The Seadragon turned slowly, ponderously, toward the gleaming point of light, her huge eyes staring fascinated. The Argan ran across the rooftops and the Seadragon followed. A cheer went up from the Silkies. The stone floated through the air for a moment as it was thrown to the next carrier and to the next. The stone raced across the rooftops, still drawing the Seadragon on. The forward Argan bounded nimbly over islands of rubble that had been left behind the Seadragon when she had first entered the city.

"That would be Handel. He's always trying to outdo Sebastian." Amadeus frowned. "Pass it on, boy. Pass it on. Don't try to outrun her."

But Handel did win the race, and he disappeared over the other side of the rubble into the open sea.

A fast boat appeared mysteriously from the south. At first we thought it was a Son of Light, but Pa looked through the binoculars. "There's an Argan at the wheel," he said in surprise.

Amadeus chuckled softly. "If a Silkie can pilot a boat, I don't see why an Argan can't."

Handel climbed into the boat and its motor revved into life. The Seadragon slithered out of the street, flattening the mound of rubble under her. Clouds of dust obscured her body as she crawled out of the city. Yard after yard of flesh swept out of the water to disappear into the dust and splash unseen back into the sea.

"The Argans have jumped out of the boat," Pa told us, and we could all see the boat leap away toward the open sea, the touchstone gleaming from its bow, a star of light that grew smaller and smaller in the night as the boat sped onward, and then vanished. The tail of the Seadragon hissed over the rocks and, with a flip, she too disappeared into the sea.

Amadeus stayed by the parapet until he heard a clicking sound from a nephew. "They're all safe then," he grunted. "Well, I suppose it's time to go home."

"I guess it is," I said, but still Amadeus did not leave. We walked along the rooftops until we were well away from the others and then sat down.

"Amadeus, you know you won't be able to stay for very long in Sheol. The city's dying."

"Who calls this Mantrap home?" Amadeus turned toward the mainland and his nostrils widened as he sniffed the air. "The wind's from the north, Tyree. Why, I can almost smell home, my real home."

"Where's that, Amadeus?"

Amadeus shook his head in amusement. "No, Manchild, almost-nephew, you know too much already."

"So this is really good-bye?"

"I'm afraid so."

I did not want to ruin the moment, and yet there had been one worry which had been nagging me for a while. This was my last chance to end it. "Please, Amadeus, just one more question before you leave."

Amadeus held up four hand-feet toward the sky. "Won't you ever give me any peace?" he said, but his expression was friendly enough. "What is it?"

"When you said that you paid your debts," I said slowly, "did that mean you took me on as a student because I was Great-Great-Grandpa's kin, or because I was a promising musician?"

"How can you ask that after the way you just played?"

"But that first time we met, I was pretty awful."

"Lord God, yes, you were"—Amadeus laughed at the memory, but it was a kind laugh—"but you weren't any worse than another beginner I knew—and your Great-Great-Grandpa never thought he was awful."

"Then you taught me for the sake of my Great-Great-Grandpa?" I said, disappointed.

"Manchild, Manchild." Amadeus hurriedly put four of his arm-legs around me, and his double hug was as strong as Pa's and yet as comforting as Ma's. It was kind of like being held by both Ma and Pa at the same time. "I did it for your sake, Manchild. I did it because you were as much of a fool as I was and still am."

Then he let go of me.

I could feel myself choking up. "Amadeus—"

Amadeus winked one eye at me. "We said our good-byes once, Tyree. That should be enough."

I got up, suddenly feeling as old and as sad as the ages. "I'll still miss you, you old Argan."

"There is nothing wrong with missing someone. Just so long as you let go." Amadeus put his hand-feet across four of his knees and rose with a small groan. "Don't forget to drop by Sheol."

"Why?" I asked without thinking. But Amadeus had already disappeared over the side without an answer. I leaned over the parapet watching the old Argan cling by his suction pads to the side of the building. A fiber shot across the street, shining with an inner light the color of sapphire. Amadeus crossed over the water easily, dropping from the line down on a slender filament and into the house across the street. He waved six of his hand-feet one last time and then he was gone.

There wasn't a Hydra left in the city—all of them had either escaped or been crushed by the Seadragon, so it was very quiet now. In the still air, in the dying night, we could hear a faint rustling. It was the wind, but it sounded as if all of Old Sion were leaving: the creatures of shadow and the ancient spirits sighing as they brushed concrete or water, whispering as they passed on, some to the shore, some to the sea. The Seadragon's voice came lonely and distant across the sea, a low moaning sound, beautiful and yet terrible. It was like music and we listened to all the sounds as a people for the last and final time.

# EPILOGUE:

## SOME LOOSE THREADS

NO ONE EVER saw an Argan after that, either in the city or on the mainland, though they say that if a man travels far enough into the northern wastelands, away from even the meanest shack, out of sight of man and water, you might hear some strange music, like a trumpet and reed pipes. But the men who tell those stories are desert prospectors who have had their brains baked hard as rocks by the sun.

Satin took his tourists back to the mainland along with all the Sons of Light who survived, settling handsome pensions on the widows—among them were Mrs. Dudum and Mrs. Gribble. At least Satin was decent about that. As for the Silkies, there was plenty of Satin's equipment to salvage in Old Sion. There were bubble-shelters, generators, motorboats, and the like as well as our own furnishings. We got some good money for them when we brought them to New Sion, and divided it among the families. We tried to stay together in Old Sion as long as we could, but it was hard enough feeding one family alone on what was left in the city, without having to feed twenty-three others. All too soon the day came when the other twenty-three families signed on with a fishing fleet that was just about to put out from New Sion.

Pa had kept one motorboat for our own use, a trim twenty-footer, and we formed a little flotilla with the skiffs surrounding our boat, moving at slow speed. Shadrach Lawson, who was with us in our boat, had become the new Captain of the Silkies. Pa tried to give him the Captain's cap and tunic but Shadrach would not take them. He said that when Pa changed his mind about trying to become a Mainlander and decided to come back to the Silkies, why, then Shadrach would step down and Pa would be the Captain again. Pa told Shadrach that he was a fool and Shadrach answered that he had been thinking the same about Pa. They laughed then and promised each other that they would keep in touch.

Poor Erasmus had not known where to go. He got seasick just looking at the water in the street, so he could not follow his Silkies out to sea, but on the other hand we had infected him with a contempt for his own native mainland. Eventually Pa had convinced Erasmus to get a teaching position near the coast, and with that compromise Erasmus had to be happy.

While we were in New Sion, Pa sent a cable down to Jubal and Poppy Hatcher, asking them if they'd put us up for a while, and they sent back an answer that they were primed and ready for us. It was good to know that we had a home waiting for us, but that did not make it any easier to leave Old Sion. We stayed on through the winter—using the winter rains as an excuse.

When Pa and I were not hunting for what game was left, we worked on the boat, getting it ready for the thousand-mile trip down the coast, while Ma and Caley dried and laid up provisions or packed what things we were taking with us. Sometimes Pa would tell me to go scavenging to see if we couldn't find something to sell to the dealers in New Sion for extra travel money. Pa knew that all the houses had been picked clean already. It was just an excuse so I could play my flute.

Spring came, bringing with it the day we had to leave Old Sion. It came too soon for all of us, though none of us said so. The day before we were to leave, Pa sent me out scavenging— for one final good-bye, I guess. I took Caley with me since I figured she would want one last ride in the skiff.

It was a strange feeling to drift along through the tall brick and stone canyons: sheer stone walls fifty feet high, soaring up out of the water to trap a narrow strip of sky. I lay back in the bow and told Caley how the sky was sliding by between the walls. It was terribly lonely and yet terribly grand to be the last humans left in Old Sion.

"Tyree," Caley said finally, "will you miss the city?"

"Of course I will," I said. "Do you miss your touch-stone?"

"Well . . ." Caley ran her fingers lightly along the side of the boat. "Do you remember that time Papa caught a song-bird?"

"Yes, I remember," I said. The songbird had been a pretty enough little bird with a metallic-blue throat and black eyes. We put it in a cage made from reeds because we had dreams of having music in the house all day long, but it only warbled for a day and then it stopped. No matter how we coaxed it and bribed it, it wouldn't do more than just stare out at the open water in the street until Pa said there were better uses for the cage.

Ma had told us then that no beautiful thing could ever be owned. It was only supposed to be in your keeping for a little while. You cherish that beautiful thing while you have it but you must be willing to give it up when it is the right time, because it was never yours to begin with.

Caley shrugged. "When you have something like the touchstone, you love it but you aren't supposed to cry when you lose it—" She added truthfully, "At least you don't let yourself cry for long."

I might complain about Caley's stubbornness sometimes—I doubt if a more cantankerous little sister could be found within a thousand light-years—but I have to admit that Caley was strong. Her inner strength might be aggravating now and then but there were times, like that moment, when I felt humble before her. "We'll find new stories just as good as the old ones," I said.

"And we'll find songs as nice as the old ones," Caley said and she leaned forward eagerly. "Sing for me, Tyree. Please?"

Suddenly I felt freer than I had in a long time. "We'll sing together," I said. We sang the old songs, the good songs, and our voices echoed and re-echoed up the silent streets. I had not been paying any attention to where we were going but unconsciously I must have been taking us to Sheol. Up till then I had held off from visiting Sheol—despite what Amadeus had advised. Somehow I had felt that finding Sheol completely abandoned would mark the end of the city for me.

"Where are we?" Caley asked.

"In Sheol," I said, and I started to tell her about the Argans, and about the things I had seen, about Amadeus, and about my class. Maybe the Argans were not there in body, but they were there in spirit. I had them and their music in my mind and in my heart; and I saw that I had something as lasting as any human can ask for.

When we reached Amadeus's house, I moored the skiff. With growing excitement, I took Caley's hand and we went inside. We found it in the rotunda waiting for us: the old Argan's egg-shaped cocoon. One end had been torn when Amadeus had re-emerged after rejuvenation, but he had carefully mended that end. I picked the cocoon up carefully and put it into Caley's arms.

She ran her fingers lightly over the fibers and the warmth of her hands made the cocoon glow for a moment where she touched it. "It's shining, Tyree, isn't it?" she asked excitedly.

"It sure is, Cal." I watched as the different colors flickered across her face, now red, now yellow, then green, and finally blue and back to red again. I was sure that this was more than just the ordinary cocoon; the Ultimate Uncle must have taken great pains to weave the fibers into a pattern. We took it and set it down on the marble. When the sunlight warmed the fibers, the cocoon shone—like rainbow casements, like the jeweled memories of a summer, like my dreams of the city— to be my music wherever we might travel.